Homecoming
Mel Teshco and Kylie Sheaffe

Homecoming
Copyright © 2022 Mel Teshco & Kylie Sheaffe
ALL RIGHTS RESERVED

Cover Art by Helzcat Designs
https://www.helzkatdesigns.com/

Chapter One

Brighton, Australia

Monday, March 21st

Robyn Newton leaned into the toilet bowl and vomited again, her belly contracting involuntarily until the sickness finally passed.

My love, why were you taken from me?

She couldn't cry anymore. She'd cried every tear out in her body, and then some. She felt cold, empty, heartsick, and disillusioned. On top of it all, she'd been fighting a guilt that ate at her, piece-by-piece.

She should have told him.

But it was too late now. Her husband had been her universe, her soul mate, ripped out of her life by a drunk, hit and run driver. She looked into the mirror. She was gaunt and hollow-eyed, her thin face haunted by the horror of the last five days.

A knock on the door sounded, followed by Marina's gentle inquiry, "Are you okay?"

Robyn took a second to respond. "Yes. I-I'll be right out."

"Okay. Take your time. I'll be waiting downstairs."

Robyn didn't answer. She was already sinking back into the quagmire of her bleak emotions, staring blankly into the mirror, waiting . . . waiting to be woken up from this nightmare.

How could he have been taken on their anniversary? How could he have been taken at all?

Her hands clenched, but she forced her trembling fingers open to adjust the collar of her lemon dress, her husband's favorite. He never had liked the color black.

She closed her eyes. It'd become a habit lately. Every time she blocked out the world, she saw her husband's face; his brilliant laughing eyes, the creases in his brow, his graying hair. But mostly, his love that had shone bright just for her.

Hugging her torso, she whispered, "I wish I could talk to you one more time, tell you how much I love you, how much I miss you. I wish I could explain how happy you made me, but mostly, I wish I could tell you that no one could replace you in my life."

She breathed in deep. The love he'd given her for so many years would keep her strong. For him, she could do this. Somehow.

Her lids flicked open as she expelled her breath. Retrieving her clutch purse from the sink, she walked slowly out of the en suite and into her bedroom, trying not to feel as the king-size bed loomed in her vision.

Leaving the main bedroom, she paused at the entrance of the study right next to the bedroom she'd shared with her husband. There had been many nights he'd burned the midnight oil in here, adding to his journal and reading. But he'd only ever been a room away.

Now . . . now he was unreachable. At least, in the physical realm.

Her husband's scent still lingered, and she inhaled the air until her breath caught on a sob. Hurrying to his big oak desk, she retrieved his bound leather journal.

She didn't have her husband with her anymore, but at least she had the book he'd poured his heart and soul into. That would have to be enough.

Heartsick, she spun away with another sob and fled from the room, closing the door behind her with a sharp snap.

Some things hurt way too much, despite the yearning.

By the time she reached the stairs, her urge to hurry was fading fast. She didn't want to leave, didn't want to face the torment ahead.

As she made her way slowly downstairs, James and Marina stepped forward to meet her, assisting her down the last few steps. She really must look as fragile and vulnerable as she felt.

Too soon they were at the church, people crammed into the pews while others stood, with her husband's casket taking center stage, almost like his death was something to be celebrated.

In some distant place in her mind she took in many of the mourners who attended, doctors and nurses who had worked at the hospital with her husband, and many of his students. In one of the pews halfway down the aisle, their, her, elderly neighbors sat alongside a middle-aged lady who'd cut her and James' hair the last ten years.

There were so many others she didn't recognize, colleagues and admirers of her husband's work. People her husband had touched in some way.

Her nails dug into the palms of her hands as she sat at the front pew, Marina and James sitting either side.

She only half-heard the minister drone on about the virtues of James Edward Newton. But what did he understand of her husband? He was reading from his notes like he would a sermon. He didn't know her husband, had no idea how good, kind, and beautiful James really was. Had been.

Journal pressed tightly against her torso, she stood, ignoring the surprised looks from Marina and James, from the packed gathering who'd come to mourn her husband.

"You'd like to say a few words?" the minister asked.

"Yes." She nodded. "Yes, I would."

She'd never been fond of public speaking but now her fears seemed achingly trivial.

The minister moved away from the pulpit and allowed her to take over. She put the journal onto the lectern. The casket, with its huge wreath of flowers, drew her stare and she had to swallow past the lump in her throat before she spoke.

"I never got a chance to say goodbye to my husband," she began hoarsely. "I never really got a chance to thank him for everything he's done for me over the years." She swept a hand towards the casket, trying not to imagine her vibrant, wonderful husband lying dead inside, trying not to think about his broken body. "But now, I have my chance."

She was vaguely aware every person in the gathering was hanging onto her every word, many of them dabbing at their eyes. It meant little to her right then. She took a breath, taking a moment to gather herself. She looked skyward. "James, my love, you were my heart. You were my soul mate, my other half. I cherished every single moment we had together. Thank you."

She heard a collective sigh from the people on the pews. She looked downward, focusing on his journal. "I'd like to share a little something from him that very few of you would know."

Opening the first page, she read her husband's handwriting.

"I saw a miracle today."

She paused, choked up. She took another breath, and then continued reading.

"My colleagues and I advised a first-time mother to say goodbye to her prematurely born daughter. We were all medically aware the tiny girl's spark of life couldn't possibly last. The Mom refused to listen. She demanded to know how we could dare suggest such a fate—that we were not God. Instead, she channeled every ounce of her determination, every ounce of her love into her baby, her baby that she touched and held at every opportunity, despite being warned not to. There was no scientific explanation for how her baby responded and fought for her little life . . . She wasn't aware that it was impossible, she was surviving . . . thriving, on the power of love. Love that my tired colleagues and I had underestimated, love that we should have offered ourselves. And hadn't. The mother sang words that were filled with love and rich with belief, words in which her baby responded. That is the kind of love that is not, and will never be, found in the barren space of a Humidicrib."

The writing blurred. Robyn looked up, memorizing the last few lines of her husband's scrawled handwriting as she finished aloud, "That was the defining moment for me, the start of much self-interrogation.

The questioning of what more I could offer in regards to scientific medicine."

An elderly gentleman a few rows back blew his nose into a large square handkerchief, but otherwise the silence was almost deafening.

Robyn closed the journal. Prisms of light poured through the stained-glass window overhead, depicting the birth of Jesus. She cleared her throat, fighting back raw emotion. "Five days ago my husband and I planned to celebrate our anniversary. Today I'm forced to say goodbye to a man who never knew he gave me something so precious, so long awaited. A miracle of our very own."

She imagined his loving face in heaven as she closed her eyes. "I was going to tell you that night. My darling. We're having a baby."

The church filled with surprised murmurs as she gathered up the journal and made her way down the two steps. She paused beside the gleaming, wood-grain casket. She laid a hand on it and whispered, "I love you." Tears flowed down her face, tears she'd mistakenly imagined were all cried out. "Goodbye, my darling."

James watched as the last of the mourners murmured their condolences to a pale but dignified Robyn before they trailed away from the professor's gravesite and to their respective cars.

He retreated a few meters, giving Robyn some space and time to grieve alone.

Grief snarled in his own belly, a sickness that threatened to swell. *Bloody hell.* How could Robyn stay so strong when all he wanted to do was scream, to rant and rave at the unfairness of it all?

Remorse hit him hard. If he hadn't given into the drugs, the professor wouldn't have come looking for him and would still be alive today. It should have been his last breath taken after the drugs he'd ingested, not the professor's.

He'd been at least partly responsible for taking away one of the world's top surgeon's. And one of the finest men a person could hope to have as a friend.

The professor's accident had left a deep void inside him, but it had also given him a conviction he never knew he possessed.

No more drugs, no more self-defeating behavior. It'd taken the professor's death to make him see the light, to see life now as a gift and something to be treasured.

The professor's death would not be in vain.

It would take one step at a time, one day at a time to overcome his drug dependency. It might be too late to win back Marina, but he'd do this. For himself. For his sister.

The time off work had been a fundamental part of the healing process, not just with the professor's death, but his own emotional blockages. He'd thrown out his stash of pills and tipped the liquor from every bottle of alcohol down the sink.

He didn't need to prove to anyone, to himself, he was strong-willed. It wasn't necessary anymore. His pill popping and his one-time binge drinking had ended for good.

Marina walked towards him, following his lead. Her stare clashed with his, hurt all too apparent in her eyes. Her grief was easily evident, but he could also decipher other emotions: abandonment, betrayal, rejection.

His heart turned over. He knew how she felt. Even knowing she was with Alexander's father, he wanted her like nothing ever before.

James released a long, slow breath. Was Marina really lost to him? Life could be taken at any moment—the professor was proof of that. But he was a fighter, clean of drugs and ready to embrace life.

He had nothing to lose . . . and yet everything to lose.

Marina looked away, hiding her too-easily-read emotions. But he didn't apologize, not right then. Besides, Marina was sure to hate him even more once he explained the reason behind his long absence, the reason he'd ignored all her phone calls and locked himself in his house, away from the world and everything in it.

He turned, glancing at the headstones with their etched words. He shook his head. A mini-bio recounting a person's lifetime, a person with a mother, a father, a family. All their worth transcribed into a stone monument.

He was only glad he'd come to understand there was more to life than just what one could see.

"So sad," Marina said softly, her voice sounding little-girl lost. "Robyn and the professor . . . they were perfect for each other."

The trees cast shadows over the headstones farther away, and James wondered at the sudden prickle of foreboding as a man in the distance stepped behind a large tree.

He pushed aside the silly apprehension, his focus returning to Marina. She'd said very little to him since this morning, where a friend had dropped her off at Robyn's house at the same time he'd pulled into the driveway.

There was much explaining to do, but a funeral wasn't the time or the place.

A light breeze picked up Marina's hair, tugging at the strands she'd pushed back into a tight bun that was losing the battle of containment. The vibrant red-gold strands were a sharp contrast to her severe, knee-length, black dress flaring out from the waist.

She looked beautiful. But it was a different kind of beautiful. She looked untouchable, distant. And a little bit scared.

He stepped towards her, searching for a safe topic. "H-how is Alexander?"

"He's good. His healthy lungs keep me awake most nights." Her face was a tight mask that slipped just a little at the mention of her son. Even so, she radiated a tension that screamed, *back off.*

Becoming aware of the slightly dark shadows under her eyes, he nodded. "You do look a little tired."

She laughed, but the sound was hollow. "Believe me, I feel it."

He ached to take her into his arms, to soothe away the strain so visible on her face. But it was no longer his right. It had probably never really been his right. "At least you have Alexander's father there, helping out."

Damn, just saying those words made his tongue thick, like he couldn't speak English.

"Roger?" Her laugh raised another few decibels, one of her hands closing into a fist over the cross she wore on a silver chain around her neck. "I wouldn't let that man near my baby if he was the last person on the planet."

James' pulse stuttered, disbelief and hope crawling through the quicksand of sorrow. "He's at home with him now though . . . isn't he?"

"No." She shook her head, scattering more hair free from its pins. "No! I put a restraining order put on him right after his unexpected hospital visit. My aunt is with Alexander. She's staying for a month to help out."

Relief warred with anxiety. He'd been so consumed by his grief he hadn't even noticed Marina's aunt next door! "A restraining order? But I thought—"

"You thought wrong." Marina's bottom lip trembled. "The bastard's been stalking me."

A protective instinct rose inside like a powerful wave. He didn't ride the emotion. He backed off. He'd play it safe and smart, not act on his compulsions.

In his peripheral, he saw Robyn turn from the graveside and approach, her head tilted high and proud, dark sunglasses concealing her red-rimmed, bleary eyes. Her hands clasping the professor's journal to her bosom conjured a déjà vu moment that reminded him of Josie and her poetry book.

Fresh guilt lanced through him. His sister was yet another loved one he'd neglected since the professor's death.

He took hold of Marina's hands. "We need to talk."

She tugged free. "I tried that already. I rang . . . I left messages on your answering machine."

"I know." He wasn't going to make excuses. "Could I drive you home?"

Her bottom lip wobbled, as if all her pent-up emotions threatened to spill free. "Thanks, but I can find my own way."

He ached to kiss her mouth, to soothe away her fears and fatigue. To help make her forget what an idiot he'd been. Instead, he reluctantly stepped back, and a moment later, offered his arm to Robyn.

The older woman managed a wan smile. "You have both been so very kind to me. It means a lot. Thank you."

"We want to be there for you, whenever you need us," Marina said huskily, falling into step beside them.

Robyn stilled beside James' car and bowed her head. James knew she held back sobs. She lifted her chin, and with surprisingly steady hands she peeled the journal from her body, holding it out to James. "My husband considered you one of his closest friends. I know . . . he'd want you to have this."

Remorse and uncertainty hit James hard. He was so unworthy of the professor's life's work. "I couldn't."

A single tear trekked past her sunglasses and down her face. "I insist." She placed a hand over her belly. "We insist."

James shoved aside self-doubts, wanting only to reassure as he accepted the book. "Thank you. I'll treasure this journal and the words inside it."

She gave an almost imperceptible nod. "I know you will. I believe you'll continue on with his good works."

"You have my word."

"There's just one condition."

"Anything."

She dabbed away the tear with a crumpled tissue. "I'd like our child to have the journal, a keepsake when he, or she, turns eighteen."

"Of course. I'll keep it safe until then."

She managed a wan smile. "Thank you."

James opened the passenger door, then shut it behind Robyn with a clunk. At the uneasy sensation crawling down his spine he looked back, past the gravestones and to the trees, where the same man stood, too far away to see him clearly.

With a frown he turned to Marina, and froze. She was staring at the man, horror etched into her face. He stepped towards her, "Marina, are you okay?"

"It's him," she whispered starkly. "It's Roger."

Shit!

His instincts had warned him earlier. It seemed he still had a way to go in learning to listen and trust in them.

He looked back, scanning the area. But Roger was already retreating like a flickering shadow amongst the far-off trees.

James drew her into his arms, holding her close. "It's okay," he said. "He's leaving." The coward. "I won't let him hurt you."

Marina stepped back, her body stiff. "I wish I could believe you." She looked away as a car pulled in behind his BMW. "My ride is here. I best get back to my son."

Had he blown all chance of being with Marina? In the past week, he'd lost a true friend and probably the woman he loved. And as he watched her walk away he had to wonder if she was walking out of his life for good.

Some hour and a half later, with the professor's journal in hand, James unlocked the front door of his house and stepped inside.

He took a deep, calming breath, trying not to imagine the every goings-on next door as he faced the empty room, trying not to envision the love filling every pore of Marina's home as he entered the tome-like quiet of his own house.

Therein lay the difference. She had a home. He had a house.

He had cleared out what had once been his liquor bar. He didn't need to prove to anyone anymore that he wasn't his father. Now he used it to store his textbooks, medical encyclopedias, paperwork, and, temporarily, Josie's poetry book.

He put the professor's journal down beside the poetry book, unable to find the will to read it right then. Not even one word. His mentor's death was still too raw, too recent.

His reserves of strength could only take him so far.

Instead, almost abstractedly, he picked up the poetry book and strode over to the recliner near the window overlooking Marina's house. He flicked on the freestanding lamp nearby. He'd read a little and keep an eye on things next door.

He opened the book and thumbed through a couple of pages. "Perfect," he mused.

Be still my friend and believe . . . the steepest path—
Your treadmill of despair is passed.
The prayer seeded in a pit of misery is known
And strength to haul your burden has grown beyond the frailest shoots
To become a sapling, sinuous and strong—roots tapped deep into the warmth of love,
Branches spreading high above, in harmony and song . . .
For you, my friend, belong.
~Sue Allen

Chapter Two

Karlcodi Mental Hospital

Monday, March 21st

A disjointed scream. The quick flash of a young woman's beautiful, terrified eyes. Another scream. Then a long, drawn out silence.

Josie's pulse jerked like a fish caught in a net. Somehow she knew she wasn't awake, even as she registered that what she was seeing, what she was hearing, had happened.

She was the invisible fabric of a past time.

"I don't want this," she said, her voice resonating eerily in her dream . . . in her mind.

But it didn't matter what she wanted. The sedation drugs Doctor Leonard had prescribed ensured she wouldn't fight her way out of the thick fog of sleep anytime soon.

Even as she grasped she was indeed dreaming, the knowledge slipped through her fingers like the long ago wisp of a memory.

Josie found herself looking down at a long wooden crate that was tacked together roughly, its crude lid lying nearby. It appeared Timothy Doore had been in all kinds of a hurry trying to conceal the body of the young woman, who appeared no older than seventeen or eighteen.

The woman who no longer made a sound.

The angelic face was made even more virtuous somehow by her neatly arranged hands, clasped prayer-like before her.

Josie felt her belly churn. No one she knew in her wing of the hospital was capable of this atrocity. And yet he'd been free to come and go. To commit this violent act.

She watched as he covered the body in a plastic sheet before nailing the lid onto the wooden crate. With a grunt of exertion, he dragged the crate outside his derelict house. It thumped down a concrete step, then he was levering one end up onto a trailer and sliding it forward.

Suddenly she was seeing him on Karlcodi grounds, throwing aside a shovel and swiping away the sheen of sweat from his brow with the back of his sleeve.

It took only minutes for him to half-drag, half-push the crate towards the wide ditch in the ground. The makeshift coffin thudded heavily into place.

No!

As the clods of dirt hit the crate, trickling their way between the wooden slats and through the gaping folds of plastic sheeting, suddenly she saw herself inside.

Her mouth filled with dirt as she tried to scream, tried to breathe. Her eyes watered at the dust and grit, made worse as she hammered the top and sides of the crate with hands that remained clasped together, locked in prayer.

Alone, terrified now beyond speech, the box within abruptly changed its dimensions. The plastic became soft, plush velvet the color of baby pink, and she wondered suddenly if she was in an outrageously expensive casket. No, much . . . much smaller.

"Somewhere Over the Rainbow" filled her ears over and over, louder and louder while she began to twirl, helplessly, dizzily, until suddenly she was no longer lying in the box, but staring down at herself, Sarah Jane's face superimposing over hers.

Fused, their features appeared doll-like, their tiny face a smudge of white porcelain against the painted, rosy red smile that was their own permanent lie. And still Josie was trapped. And still she was alone.

"Help me!"

She woke with a loud gasp.

It's only a dream. It's only a dream. It's only a dream.

Except, no matter how many times she might try to convince herself, she knew deep down at least some of it wasn't. The trick would be now sorting the wheat from the chaff, the real-life from the cameo roles of the mind.

"Ah, you're awake," Tess said, putting down her chart with a warm smile. "You were out for some time."

Josie didn't respond, too fraught and wrung out to make polite conversation.

Undaunted, Tess continued. "All the other patients are up and about. Matt asked for you. He's waiting in the common room."

"James. Where's James?" Josie managed, hating the unknown fear lodged like a stone in her belly. She'd warned him of danger, had felt it like a hot breath on her face. And now . . . now he hadn't visited her for almost a week. It wasn't like him at all.

A week she'd had to finally come to terms with the fate of her brother. She could no longer save the world, could no longer save James. She'd reluctantly accepted that now, and with that acceptance had come an inner peace she embraced with everything she had.

"James rang earlier. We told him you were sleeping. He said he'd be in tomorrow." She gave a sad shake of her head. "He said to let you know he lost a dear friend, Professor James Newton, in a car accident."

Josie felt the stone in her belly slip away as though it'd never been. "Blue car splattered red. It was his car," she whispered.

Tess raised a brow. "I'm not sure what you mean, Josie?"

Josie smiled. "It's okay. I do."

With Tess clucking over her like a mother hen, helping her wash and dress, and then walking with her to the common room, Josie had the ever-growing impression that change was on its way.

Karlcodi is no longer your home. You don't need Karlcodi anymore.

"Molly?" she asked, feeling like an excited little girl whose best friend had just returned from a long journey. Peering around and seeing no one, she asked louder, "Molly?"

Shh.

Tess clucked her tongue. "Now, Josie, you're not seeing Molly again, are you?"

Josie cast Tess a look as they traversed the corridor. She shook her head. "No. No, I'm not."

I'm not seeing her at all. Molly's white energy is too weak with Timothy's darkness overpowering it. But at least I'm hearing her now.

Tess smiled approval. "I'm glad. I think you're getting much better. In fact, I'm going to note that on my report to the doctor."

Josie nodded. "Yes. Thank you. H-he'll sign my release today."

As Josie walked into the common room, she heard Tess mutter thoughtfully, "I doubt that."

Matt was alone and sitting in his usual spot at the table, staring at a pack of cards in his hands. He looked up at her approach and smiled. "Hi, J-Josie."

She smiled back. Though he'd inadvertently hurt her with his tarot cards—his past trauma—she was going to miss Matt.

She was never coming back to Karlcodi. She knew that now without Molly's voice whispering in her mind. The task she'd been set by someone much higher than she was drawing to its conclusion.

Matt took the regular, nondescript playing cards out of his pack. He placed card after card on top of one another, each slightly down from the one underneath so that the suit of each card could be seen . . . heart after heart after heart.

He must have arranged them that way, surely? She could tell he was comfortable with the energy revealed . . . and so was she. On a soft sigh, she asked, "Where are your tarot cards?"

Matt quickly gathered his cards up and shuffled them, his face tight. "Doctor L-Leonard t-t-took them from me." He divided the deck in half, and then allowed the facing ends of the split cards to fall one on top of the other, interweaved. He pushed them together, making the deck whole again.

Holding out the shuffled pack he said, "Ch-choose one." At her hesitation, he added, "P-p-please."

She nodded. She knew which card he wanted her to pull out—a queen—but she was drawn to another like a bird to its roost. He indicated she place it face-up before him. When she revealed the king of clubs, his face went ashen, his chest heaving as he sucked in air.

Immediately Josie understood. His physical response was exactly how she'd reacted in the past to his tarot card readings. Except she no longer absorbed his negative energy. She was shielded, ready.

It appeared that fully accepting and embracing her gift, which many considered a curse, had allowed its true colors to shine whilst unlocking the ability to control the forces she'd had little power over before.

She leaned over the table and plucked the king of clubs from his view. She pushed it back into the deck and then flipped through the pack until she found a queen of hearts. Placing it face-up before him, she felt his instant calm.

"Th-thank you," he said hoarsely.

She nodded and sat beside him, their comfortable silence a bonding of friendship forged by understanding, mutual trust, and respect.

But the peaceful vibe was shattered by an abrupt shift in the air, the negative energy of Timothy Doore. He materialized right behind Matt, peering over his shoulder and taking a look at the queen of hearts.

Timothy's evil force no longer terrified her. Not only did she now have a confidence in her own abilities, she knew of his remorse, his guilt, and eternal suffering.

"It's so c-c-cold in here," Matt said, feeling the vibe but blessedly unaware of the presence in the room.

Timothy pointed at Matt. He wanted to show her something. She nodded. And though she was still in the room, still subliminally aware of everything around her, she was seeing another time, another place.

She was Matt . . .

He pressed shaky hands over his ears, trying to block out the almost continual fighting of his parents through the paper-thin walls. He needn't have bothered. Nothing could stop them now. He bit back a sob. Nothing could stop the terror clawing at his innards with sharp, taloned hands.

It was bitterly cold outside, a dank winter's evening on the family's dairy farm just outside Melbourne. And yet, sweat dripped off his brow.

It wouldn't be long now. The violence was building and soon he'd feel the wrath of his dad.

His mother's voice was cajoling, trying hopelessly to crack her husband's rigid stance. "C'mon, George, he's just finding his way, that's all. He's a good kid if you'd just give him a chance."

"He's gay!" George spat the word out as though it was acid on his tongue. "You know that, I know that! Damn it, woman, he hangs out with girls he doesn't even date, not like a man does. He cares more about his hair and his nails than you do."

"I know," his mother all but whimpered.

"The son of my own loins, and he doesn't even watch bloody rugby!"

Matt couldn't hold back the sobs then. They shook his shoulders as he curled up on his creaky bed, waiting for the inevitable flogging that was to come. Once his dad spoke about rugby—he'd been a star player in his heyday—there'd be hell to pay. No son of his chose drama classes over sports.

A glass shattered against the wall, undoubtedly his dad's empty beer bottle. "I'll flog every bit of gayness out of the boy," he rasped.

"Don't hurt him," his mother yelled as his father's heavy tread sounded down the hallway. But they all knew she wouldn't try to stop her husband. That deep down she blamed her son for the fights, the upheavals.

The door flung open, banging loudly against the wall. The light switch clicked on, the naked bulb glaring bright. "On your feet, boy."

Matt openly sobbed now, great shuddering sobs he couldn't stop, couldn't control. And as sudden warmth seeped between his thighs, he shook his head. "I c-c-can't."

"Shut your mouth, boy, and get on your feet. Now!"

Somehow Matt found his legs supported him. George's bloodshot eyes widened as he saw the wet pajama bottoms. "You pissed your pants, boy?"

"Y-y-yes."

His father's head fell back, laughter spewing from his fleshy lips. He stopped abruptly, any fun to be found at his son's expense soon dissipating. "You really are a pansy, aren't you?" He didn't wait for a reply. "I'll put a stop to that, boy."

Suddenly they were in the barn. A rope had been tied to the rafters. "No more beatings, no more threats. This is the real deal, boy."

Matt struggled ineffectually against his father's beefy grip. "Please, no, d-d-don't."

His dad dragged him over to the rope, fumbling with the noose before fitting it tightly over his neck. "Your choice, boy. Life as a man, or death as a freak."

Josie jerked once as the vision abruptly cleared. Timothy Doore watched her for a couple of seconds before turning to walk towards the common room door, his dark form disappearing into thin air.

Josie understood. Timothy wanted to redeem himself, wanted to right all his wrongs. It was too late for Sarah Jane, but it wasn't for Matt.

She turned to Matt and took hold of his hand. "I'm sorry for what your father did to you," she said. "He had no right . . . no right at all."

Matt looked at her with stunned, dawning comprehension. And then, like an explosion waiting to happen, he savagely swiped the cards off the table. They fluttered to the floor like feathers falling from a slit pillow. When one card landed face-up, she saw Matt's fury plummet into utter despair. With his face pressed into his outspread hands, he cried like a baby.

Josie put her arm around his shaking shoulders. She didn't need to see the card to know it was the king of clubs. Matt had an uncanny ability to deal the same card over and over, his fate sealed in his past.

"What the hell is going on in here?"

Josie raised her head at Doctor Leonard's sharp tone, reading his hostility in every stiff line of his big body. She frowned. He was still a big man, but he'd lost quite a bit of weight recently, his face drawn and lined.

"The cards are reading Matt's past so that he can live his future," she said a little defiantly but Doctor Leonard clearly wasn't in any frame of mind to be reasonable and open-minded.

"What are you talking about now?"

She turned to Matt, asking gently, "Do you mind?" At his almost imperceptible, jerky nod, she turned back to the doctor. "Matt as a young boy was badly abused."

The doctor's nostrils flared, and he looked all of a cat with its fur stroked backwards. "I'm well aware of Matt's history, Josie, thank you."

Her chin tilted. "Oh? Did you know his dad tried hanging him for being gay?"

"Don't be ridiculous! Matt has told me on a number of occasions the close relationship he shared with his father. You cannot go around making up such stories," the doctor snapped. "I think I'd be more qualified to know about Matt's past, don't you?"

Though she couldn't see Molly, Josie felt her weak presence. She closed her eyes, blocking out her other senses to focus on Molly's whispered words.

Matt's father threatened him. Said he'd kill Matt's mother then him, if he ever told.

When Josie flicked her eyelids open, her stare didn't swerve from the doctor's narrowed, speculative gaze. "Trust me in this," she said, "Matt won't get better until he can let go of the terrible energy he harnesses within himself."

"Josie, Josie, Josie." The doctor clucked his tongue. "Look at Matt. Can't you see you made him regress? Do you call that better?"

"He'll get worse before he gets better. It's part of the healing process."

The doctor's scorn turned to furious disbelief, his face beet-red. "What are you, his doctor now?"

"No. I care about him." Her chin lifted. "Besides which, it's commonsense."

"You're really something, you know that?" There was not an ounce of praise in his voice. "Not only do you undermine everything I've worked hard for all my life, but you shove hope down a person's throat until they almost choke on their own self-doubts."

The doctor shook his head. "You even had me doubting myself over your outrageous claims, making me put two-and-two together and imagining for a minute it came to four. But then I realized that not one of your claims has ever been substantiated and I needed to remind myself you're in a hospital because of your delusions and mental state." He crossed his arms and drew himself to his full height. "I suggest in future you keep your thoughts to yourself."

Matt started rocking in his chair, his arms crossed with his hands on his shoulders as he babbled, "He-he's g-g-going to k-kill me. D-Daddy's going to k-kill me. J-Josie's right. D-D-Daddy will kill me."

Doctor Leonard paled at Matt's admission. Spinning on his heel, he lurched over to the window overlooking the gardens and shed outside. His whole body shook with impotent fury and grief, and more than a little denial.

Josie couldn't help Matt right then, despite the fact their energies were tuned into the same frequency. Instead she followed Doctor Leonard over to the window, feeling strength within her she never had felt before. And it suddenly occurred to her that having to stand alone, not having Molly to guide her, had made her a far stronger person.

She stilled beside him and explained, "I finally know what I've been born to do, why I've been put here from the very beginning."

He stiffened, and she looked up, following his gaze to the shed outside.

It was almost eerily still outside. But they were both aware of the sudden breeze that bent the tops of the rose bushes sideward. Rose petals whirled through the air, round and round, hovering for a moment then tossed like confetti in a spurt of wind towards the shed.

Doctor Leonard's jaw dropped open.

Josie touched his arm. "Your daughter just gave you a sign. You know what you have to do."

*

James woke to the feel of grass underneath his body and the sound of birdsong overhead. He blinked a few times, trying to make sense of his surroundings.

He wasn't in his bed at home that was for sure. White headstones were his companions, and nearby, the freshly turned earth of the professor's burial site.

"Oh, shit!"

He scrambled onto his feet, swiping a hand through his hair and waiting for his clamoring senses to settle. How did he get here? Was he hallucinating? Dreaming?

Only one thing was certain right then. If he wanted to find peace he had to trust in himself, in these too-real visions.

The peculiar but powerful sensation of being watched swept through him once again. He spun on his heel, scanning left and right but seeing nothing but headstones shimmering bright beneath the sun. Plastic flowers and wilted, once-fresh flowers jostled for prime position on their tiny pieces of real estate.

It appeared he was alone. He knew he wasn't. "What do you want from me?" he shouted. "Show me what it is you need me to do!"

A dog barked. Movement caught his eye. He stared hard. "Josie?"

She stepped into plain view, Rocco by her side. Her stare was unwavering, beckoning.

He stepped forward, frowning. He perceived she wanted him to follow her, but surely not away from the professor's grave? The professor's death was what these dreams had all been leading up to, wasn't it?

Josie turned and the dog followed, his tail waving like a feather duster behind him as they made their way through the maze of headstones.

"Wait." He jogged after them, keeping them in his sight but unable to gain any ground.

His sister and Rocco headed directly towards the cremation wall, where Josie stilled beside a weeping woman in her own world of emotional pain.

Josie glanced behind her, apparently ensuring he'd followed. With a sad smile, she abruptly disbanded into a waft of smoke, her wispy form then pouring into one of the boxes in the wall.

James felt his heart thud in something too close to a panic attack. He forced himself to remain calm. He could handle this without pain medication to dull his faculties. He just had to trust in himself.

Rocco's tail drooped and he let out a distressed whine. And suddenly James wasn't sure if Rocco's anxiety was from Josie's disappearance or the woman sobbing close by.

She raised her head, swiping at her tears and staring at the wall, appearing totally oblivious to his presence.

He stepped closer, frowning. "Mother?" he whispered.

The woman was his prim and proper and emotionless mother. She was on her knees, her spine bent and defeated, her head clasped in her hands and her shoulders shaking with grief.

He'd never seen her cry, much less lose control. He could scarcely comprehend she was kneeling in the grass in her pristine stockings, let alone the fact she was here at all and so visibly distraught.

"I reckon that woman could wake the dead."

James started with alarm, twisting around at the too-familiar voice and glimpsing the dark-skinned face of Baxter beneath his felt hat.

James woke abruptly, his hands curled into fists and his cheeks wet with tears. Guilt lanced him deep. He'd been too high even to attend Baxter's funeral.

His open lounge room window showcased the lightened night sky streaked with the soft pink and gold of dawn. Baxter's presence lingered, his unmistakable voice whispering, "Goodbye, my friend."

A lump clogged James' throat. "Goodbye, Baxter."

He understood this unfinished business with Baxter—but his mother?

Josie's poetry book was still on his lap, the lamp casting a pool of light across the pages.

His eyes narrowed as he slowly exhaled. This wasn't the poem he'd read earlier. This was something else entirely.

When I am glum, the light repressed with grimy fog
Settles thick around my neck—a misery I cannot check
Descends from brightest, bluest sky—I lift my head as though to breathe
My arms so leaden I can't heave the weight from pushing down on me—
Thick, grey army blanket—sea of sodden wool, pulling me under,
And I wonder . . . why today?
When that sodden blanket lifts, this wondrous world, full of gifts—
Sunshine jewels on spider threads, blossoms with their nodding heads,
Everything is such a joy!
The planet spinning past my eyes;

And others who might not surmise my changing moods would never think—
That on the toss of a coin,
Or passing blink
Of a teardrop on lashes,
My world could turn to ashes,
But it does . . .
~Sue Allen

A soft breeze whispered against James' skin, flicking over a couple of pages. He stood and closed the window, feeling more than a bit foolish.

It had only been the wind.

Chapter Three

Clifton Hill, Australia

Saturday, April 23rd

Leonard moved restlessly from room to room in his multi-level townhouse. He paused on the landing. Before him, on the rose-colored wall, hung a large family portrait. The house had once been filled with love and laughter. Now it echoed with nothing more than his footsteps.

He'd never felt more alone.

He forced his limbs into motion.

It'd been—what?—almost five weeks, since Josie had last mentioned Sarah Jane and her being buried beneath the hospital shed. Five weeks of pure, soul-destroying torture. Even food that had once seemingly filled the void within held no interest to him anymore.

His clothes hung off him now, but he was too exhausted and disinterested to care. He'd tightened his belt another couple of notches, pretending an enjoyment he didn't feel at the air circulating beneath his too-large shirts.

He stopped beside the door to Sarah Jane's bedroom. It had been closed—since the day his wife had left—the memories within too much to bear. He sucked in a wobbly breath, pushed the door open and flicked on the light.

Apart from a layer of dust, nothing had changed within the room. It looked as it'd always looked, but now instead of being a sanctuary for Sarah Jane, it was little more than a shrine to her.

She had been a real girly-girl, from what she wore to what she'd helped choose for her bedroom.

Had been?

He shook his head. He couldn't go there right now, maybe not ever. Instead he soaked in Sarah Jane's décor with a heart-rending nostalgia that was almost masochistic. Everything in here represented a memory, a real-life event linked to his daughter.

The teardrop white crystal chandelier was a carefully selected graduation gift from him and his wife. He bit back a sob. Sarah Jane had never even got to see its sparkling lights.

Her candy-pink comforter with matching tasseled cushions and pillows was a twelfth birthday gift from Sarah Jane's Nan, who was paradoxically still alive and kicking at the ripe old age of eighty-nine.

Propped against the cushions was Sarah Jane's huge teddy bear dressed in a pink tutu and ballet slippers. He'd won it for her at a carnival when they'd holidayed in a small town on the northern coast. His daughter had treasured that teddy bear far beyond any of the expensive trinkets he'd bought her over the years.

His gaze automatically veered to the white dresser, where the music box he'd bought her from Tiffany's still resided.

His vision distorted as he found the strength to stride across the pristine cream carpet. He smoothed a hand through the dust, over the still glossy surface of the music box. And somehow he withheld the maelstrom of emotions within as his wife's bitter words replayed in his head.

All Sarah Jane ever saw was the little wind-up ballerina, trapped inside the box, all alone.

He broke down, tears pouring down his cheeks as he wept, "Why? Why us?"

He caught sight of his reflection in the mirror. He flinched, despising what he'd become. "Look at me," he choked out, scrubbing a hand over his eyes, "haggard and wasting away. Talking to myself as if I were one of my patients." He shook his head. "I really am going crazy."

Something shifted behind his stare. He frowned, peering a little harder. His eyes . . . they were no longer his.

His heart bounced in his chest, shock suspending him from belief for a couple more beats. A youthful blue gaze, so very sad, watched him from his own reflection.

It couldn't be.

"Sarah Jane?" he croaked.

His image blurred and warped. Became hers. He froze. Though conscious of her bright fuchsia graduation dress, her upswept golden hair and outer loveliness, he immediately recognized the ethereal sadness radiating from within.

He lurched forward. But as he touched the cold glass, the reflection instantly became him.

"My angel, don't go," he whispered. "My sweet, sweet angel." Tears blurred his vision.

Why had she come to him now? What was she trying to tell him?

He sagged. His shoulders trembled then shook hard as grief welled inside. He couldn't deny it any longer.

Josie was right. His little girl was never coming back.

"Damn it all to hell!" He shoved the music box off the dresser. It clattered onto the floor, a couple of long, drawn-out notes reverberating from its unhinged lid.

His daughter dead . . . even now it seemed almost inconceivable. But her appearance tonight confirmed his worst fears.

It wasn't the first time he'd felt her near, felt her presence. And ignored her. To admit she was near would admit she was dead. "I'm so sorry, Sarah Jane," he said aloud, "so very, very sorry for not being there for you."

He retrieved the music box, the ballerina within lying on its side. Still. Quiet. He only hoped his Sarah Jane was someplace happy and peaceful, a place full of her own rainbows.

Comprehension dawned, a mind-numbing fog lifting like it'd never been. He returned the music box to where it belonged on the dresser and backed out of the room to the doorway. "Is that it?" he asked hoarsely, searching the empty room. "You're trapped here?"

Then it hit him.

The music James had heard. The maps Josie had drawn long before his daughter's death. The rose petals blowing on the breeze. They really were all signs.

Resolve filled him. He couldn't risk it, couldn't take the chance he wasn't hearing her. Not anymore.

It was past time he believed in the inconceivable and thought beyond science. It was time he eliminated any possibility she was buried under Karlcodi's shed.

First thing in the morning he'd call a contractor.

On edge and more than a little strung out, he swallowed a couple of sleeping pills. He placed his empty glass of water onto the sink with a *clack,* before turning with a savage curse towards his liquor cabinet. He poured himself an aged malt whiskey. Tossing back the amber liquor, he refilled the glass to its rim and carried it with him to his secluded rooftop terrace.

He'd felt close to her out there. Now . . . now he knew why.

His heart clenched. He'd once spent many a time here entertaining with his family. The views were glorious. Though daylight showcased a panoramic and uninterrupted outlook of Melbourne's CBD and the distant ranges, right then it was a black sea of twinkling lights.

He looked up. Countless stars studded the night sky, and he wondered for one crazy moment which one of them was Sarah Jane. He raised his glass and his voice cracked as he vowed, "My angel, I'll leave no stone unturned to find you, leave nothing to chance to set you free."

Swallowing the last of his drink, he made his way downstairs. He turned on the television and sank into his big armchair. He really should have a shower and something to eat. Both seemed like too much effort.

The sleeping pills were already doing their job. His earlier restlessness was rapidly growing into bone-deep tiredness.

With half an ear, he registered the drone of the late night news.

A young woman's body has been found late this afternoon in a shallow grave in bush land close to Melbourne. It is believed the body has been buried there for at least six years.

But even as despair ate further into his soul, weariness swept over him before he found the strength to change channels.

Leonard glanced down at his notes, then back up to his patient. He frowned at Timothy, tapping his gold pen against the chart. "According to your last doctor's notations you suffered a violent relapse just days after release." He raised a brow. "You assaulted a young woman?"

Timothy's face flushed, shame tattooing his expression. "Doctor Darnoel changed my drugs." He bit his lip, his eyes downcast. "I started hearing the voices again. They wouldn't stop."

Leonard frowned, unsettled by Timothy's statement and the odd note he'd never before heard thicken his voice. "Voices? You never said anything to me about voices."

"I didn't?"

Leonard shook his head, distracted by the odd swirling red and purple sunset outside Karlcodi's window and puzzled why he should find that not quite right.

Timothy jumped up and down in his seat, clapping his hands like an excited five-year-old watching a dolphin show.

He stilled, but that same light of enthusiasm glittered behind his eyes. "I hear them all the time, but they are much worse when I'm not medicated."

The swirling red and purple grew into waves, curling up and over before crashing onto the shore. The colors drizzled away in a sickly, muddied green and orange. He refocused on Timothy. "Well, we won't be putting you back on those pills anytime soon."

Timothy breathed out a big sigh. "Thank you. I'd hate to give into temptation again." He giggled at something, as though sharing a joke. He nodded agreement and looked up. Something . . . disturbing now lit up his eyes. "And I'd hate to disturb my roses."

Leonard felt his frown momentarily deepen. What the hell was Timothy talking about? And who in hell was he talking to? He cleared his throat, but oddly, his fears slid away as he said, "I hear you have a deft touch with the gardens."

Karlcodi's roses had never looked better since Timothy had volunteered his services.

Leonard managed a faint smile. "The head gardener has already sung your praises."

Timothy grinned, but his white smile was now black, his teeth rotten stumps, and all his shame dropping away like it'd never been. "It's all in the fertilizer."

Crimson rose petals, as bright as blood droplets, fluttered through the air all around them. Leonard didn't blink. He felt his smile stretch even as his stomach spun sickly.

The words Timothy spoke didn't quite ring true, though he was surely sincere? He nodded carefully. "I trust you, Timothy. Yes, I trust you."

Leonard jerked awake with a gasp. The nightmare had been so real, so vivid. But what did it all mean . . . the rose petals, the innuendo about the fertilizer . . . ?

Damn Josie and her deranged visions! She'd infected his head, caused too many doubts to manifest in his mind.

Had he done the right thing signing Josie's release form five weeks ago? He shook his head. Of course he had, but once again he was looking for someone to blame, instead of thank.

He pushed onto his feet, uncaring dawn was only just breaking. It was time to settle this, once and for all.

After making some phone calls, he finally rang James. It had been the young doctor and his sister who had taken his blinkers off. They needed to be there. "James," he greeted, "I've organized a crew to demolish the shed and—" His voice broke a little. "—dig up the footings. I'd like you and Josie to be there too."

On the other end of the line James let loose an expletive and asked, "Are you serious? What if—?"

Leonard grimaced, ignoring the waves of nausea in his belly and cutting James short. "There's no room in my life for 'what if's' anymore, James. I owe it to Sarah Jane to eliminate every possibility."

No matter how implausible.

James let out a weary sigh. "Of course. We'll see you there soon."

*

Josie followed James from his car, to where the shed's excavation had begun. She clutched her poetry book in her chilled hands.

She slowed, soaking in the electric atmosphere. The energy was strong here, so powerful it all but crackled the air.

She stopped beside James and stared at what had once been the garden shed. The building had been knocked down, an excavator now grappling with the concrete slab, breaking it up and prizing it from the ground.

Doctor Leonard turned to her and said carefully, "I'm glad you came."

Josie met his stare. He looked terrible. Ill. A mere shadow of the big man he'd once been. She managed a nod. "I wouldn't miss saying goodbye to Sarah Jane."

James shifted from foot to foot, clearly made uncomfortable by her comment, and at the direction the conversation was going.

The doctor's jaw tightened. "Josie, as much as a part of me wishes otherwise, nothing will be found here, proving beyond any reasonable doubt—"

The bucket on the machinery clanked. The operator leaned out of the cabin and yelled, "We've hit something. Looks like some kind of wooden trunk."

The doctor paled, swaying as he slowly turned around. "It can't be," he whispered.

Josie brushed past him, her brother moving swiftly to her side. He let out a taut breath. She tucked the poetry book under one arm and took hold of his hand, linking her fingers through his.

She glanced at him, seeing in his wide stare all the rational and logical ideals of the past shattered in this one moment.

She squeezed his hand in silent understanding.

Leonard lurched forward, his throat convulsing as though he were choking on his own words. "Tell me that wispy smoke is coming out of the machinery and not from the trunk!" He collapsed onto his knees, caring less about a response as he croaked, "Sarah Jane, is it possible? My . . . Sarah Jane?"

Josie turned to the doctor and gently explained, "It's not smoke, and it's not coming from the machinery. But it is Sarah Jane." She paused. "She's not alone. See? There are two columns . . . two spirits."

Doctor Leonard jerked back in alarm. "Yes," he whispered starkly. He clasped his hands together. "I see!"

Josie nodded. "They are both released now, free to move on."

Opening up to the doctor's psyche, she experienced his every emotion and was well aware of his growing rage, his disbelief at Timothy's connection to Sarah Jane. But she understood his reaction.

The doctor ran clenched fingers along his scalp. "He . . . he won't follow Sarah Jane, will he?"

"No, I don't believe so. Timothy has his own journey to take. And Sarah Jane . . . she is an angel."

"Then I can let my little girl rest in peace," the doctor said, swiping away his tears with trembling hands. "I can say goodbye until we meet again."

Josie smiled. Yes, Sarah Jane was at peace, but Doctor Leonard would soon be, too. At long last he had acknowledged the truth. He had closure. He could live again.

She squeezed James' hand before releasing hold and opening her poetry book. She asked the doctor, "May I read a poem for Sarah Jane . . .? She loves poetry."

The doctor nodded, then said brokenly, "Sh-she did."

James shook with emotion as he wrapped an arm around Josie's waist, pulling her close in a brotherly show of support and pride. She let out a slow breath, for the first time in her life truly feeling accepted.

At the edge of her vision the dense gray of Timothy's spirit slowly dissipated, already leaving this world. Sarah Jane's energy grew brighter, more radiant, now shining in a rainbow of colors.

She smiled at the unexpectedly beautiful sight, smoothing a hand over the page she'd marked four days ago for this very event. She hadn't needed to hear any voices in her head to know in advance this day was coming.

"What's going on?" the machine operator asked, clearly baffled by the huddle of people standing close to the hole in the ground. Obviously this man was immune to the phenomenon going on right in front of him.

Doctor Leonard motioned with his hand. "Take a break, leave us for a bit."

Josie took a breath and began to read.

My darling, when you look at me with anger in your eyes,
Fierce resentment banishing your innocent surprise,
It fills my very being with excruciating pain,
Crumpled with emotion as you eye me with disdain.
And yet, beneath this torrid storm, an ocean wells with love;
An undercurrent far below those troubled waves above . . .
For I am still your father, and you, my dearest girl,
Are all that is important in this vibrant throbbing world!
Deeper, flows my love for you, than choppy fragile waves,
Which ebb and flow eternally in ever-passing days.
My passion sings in darkest depths, above the ocean floor;

Paternal and instinctive, I will love you ever more.
I love you as you smile at me with tears upon your face;
Indignant as you contemplate the failing human race . . .
I love you as no other can, no matter what you do—
For I am still your father and I'm always here for you.
~Sue Allen

Chapter Four

Carlton, Australia

Saturday, April 23rd

James pulled into his driveway, still unable to speak of the surreal event he'd witnessed.

Josie, never big on words at the best of times, had left him to his silence. She'd known better than anyone the need to absorb the unreality that was her world.

How had his sister ever coped? How had she lived with these visions, these nightmares with so few believing what she saw, what she heard? Bloody hell, her own parents—his parents—had turned on her!

Guilt knifed inside him.

He'd never believed her. Not really.

He unclipped his seatbelt and twisted in his seat to face her. "Are you okay?

She smiled, and he realized she was different somehow. No longer a fragile, frightened little girl clinging to her beliefs. Yes, he'd seen a change in her ever since she'd left Karlcodi five weeks ago, but now there was steel, a new strength in her proud stare.

"James, I do believe I've never felt better."

Relief filled him. Was it possible Josie was complete now? That she'd found a place to belong, a place of peace? He climbed out of the car, linking his arm through hers as they moved towards his house.

Since he'd allowed his sister—with more than his fair share of reservations—to move into his house from Karlcodi, they'd become closer than they ever had before.

He attributed much of Josie's mental healing to his neighbor. Marina had welcomed his sister into her home, into her heart, encouraging Josie with her violin practice. James could hardly fathom just how far Josie had come in her musical abilities in so short a time.

He glanced next door. He only wished things between himself and Marina was as great. But his beautiful neighbor had been burned one too many times.

At the front door, Josie turned to him. "Why don't you go to her, James?" When he threw her a disbelieving frown, she added gently, "I'm so proud of you. You haven't had one single pill in the five weeks I've been here. It's time you proved yourself to Marina. Besides, she needs you right now."

He blew out a breath, and then nodded. "You're right. This has gone on long enough. If I have to beg for her forgiveness, I will."

As he strode back the way he'd just come, he heard Josie whisper, "I know what I have to do."

He shrugged off her words. He'd question his sister on that later. Right now . . . he had some begging to do.

When Marina opened the door even before James lifted his hand to knock, he guessed that she'd seen him approach, or even better, had been waiting for him to finally get the nerve to come over. Powerful feelings rushed over him like waves, one after the other, as he gazed at her. "Hi, Marina," he said softly.

"Hi."

She looked tired and a little gaunt. The antithesis to how he felt since being off the drugs.

"I just wanted—"

"It's been a—"

They stopped talking simultaneously. He held her stare for a couple of beats, before both of them burst into sudden laughter.

Marina stepped aside. "Come in, please." Then clearing her throat, she added, "Actually I'm glad you called in. I wanted you to meet my Aunt Kaye before she leaves."

James' couldn't stop the wide smile spreading over his face as he stepped passed her. He'd truly, deeply missed her.

But would she ever trust him enough to think he wouldn't let her down again? That the pull of drugs wouldn't prove too strong?

Her aunt turned in her seat beside the lounge window, her hands stilling in the act of carefully wrapping her tarot cards into their silk cloth.

"Aunt Kaye, I'd like you to meet my neighbor, James."

Her aunt appraised him, her blue gaze shrewd. "So this is the young man causing you so much grief?"

Marina shook her head. "You'll give James the wrong idea." She turned to him. "I haven't been darkening your name, I promise." She swept a hand towards the tarot cards. "Aunt Kaye did a reading for me. You, ah, you featured prominently."

James couldn't help but wonder what else her aunt had foretold, but going by Marina's expression it must have mostly good news. Still, he had caused Marina grief and he wasn't about to pretend otherwise.

James lifted a hand to Marina, before dropping it by his side. "I know it sounds cliché, but I honestly never meant to hurt you." He turned to Kaye. "Marina and Alexander deserve the very best. It's why I've been soul searching, seeking answers I was once too afraid to learn."

Marina's eyes brightened with hope, then flickered with uncertainty. But she searched his stare, as if aware of the clean, clear depths. She pulled her gaze away from him, back to her aunt's no-nonsense expression. "The cards don't lie, young man," Kaye announced, raking him with a crafty look behind her oversized glasses. "Seems it's your turn for a reading."

James frowned. Only as he Marina smiled encouragement did his qualms turn into steadfast resignation. "You'll stay?" he asked her.

Marina nodded. "Of course, if that's what you want."

He gave a rather sheepish shrug. "It is."

He took a seat opposite Kaye at her silk-covered card table. Sandalwood incense sharpened the air, the flame of a burned-down candle flickering on the window ledge. Marina moved to stand behind him.

"Shuffle the cards," Kaye instructed him, "and whenever you're ready, stack them into three piles. Past. Present. And future."

Kay flipped a card over from the top of one of the three piles. "Hierophant," Kaye said. "He represents your past. He is the healer Chiron. Wise priest. The scroll he carries is the scroll of the law, the written word which through revelation communicates the will of the divine."

"What does it all mean?"

Kaye studied the layout. "As you have drawn this as a past card, I assume this person has tried to seek answers of a philosophical nature. Maybe he's discussed his problems with a priest as he feels he needs some guidance to lead him to the future."

She turned the next card over. "This card is your present. Ah, the magician. He is the god Hermes, guide of travelers, patron of thieves and liars, ruler of magic and bringer of luck."

James leaned forward, caution falling away as an eagerness to learn instead rose from within. "That's good news then?"

Kaye frowned, contemplative. "It seems a person in your life has hidden talents. But their new journey is possible only if they develop their talent further, by looking deeper within oneself."

Flipping the last card, she murmured, "The future. Death. He is the dark god, Hades, Lord of the underworld. I interpret this as infinite change, of things coming to an end."

"More death?" His voice cracked.

"Not always death. Often the end of things as we've known them. A great change." Kaye shrugged. "But whether or not the end is painful depends upon the person's capacity to accept and recognize its necessity. An opportunity for a new life possible as the old one is let go."

James sat straighter. "It makes sense. Are they, the cards, telling you anything else?"

Kaye stayed silent for a moment, and Marina knew she was gathering the images in her head, the vocal cues. "There is a blond girl, and the letter 'M.'"

"Not Josie, then?"

Kaye frowned. "I've seen Josie. But no. No. It's her, but not her. No, I'm certain it's not. She's not of this world." Kaye nodded. "She sends her love."

James nodded. "I see."

Marina fidgeted behind him, as though wishing to talk.

Kaye didn't seem to notice. She thought a little more, then said, "Your soul sings now . . . you are no longer sleepwalking." She watched him carefully. "Does that make sense?"

James sat back a little, his knee beginning to bounce on its own volition, his hands clenching and unclenching together beneath the coffee table. Conversely, he was aware Marina had stiffened behind him, as if what he said next was of the utmost importance.

Perhaps it was?

Marina knew as well as he did that Kaye referred to his 'gifts' that were no longer bound tight by the drugs he'd taken.

He released a long, slow breath. "Yes. I think it does."

Kaye nodded. "You are destined for great things, for doing things of value."

Kaye glanced at each of the cards, then looked away, staring at the blank dining room wall, as if gathering her thoughts. "There is a thin, older woman, narrow-minded with a steely spine. She stares at a clock. With each tick, she is fading out sight."

James leaned forward again, his internal antennae switching into high alert. "I dreamed I saw my mother at the cemetery. She was crying." He shook his head, his shoulders slumping. "Sorry, it was just a dream, probably nothing."

"You being here isn't nothing, you having the dream and asking me about isn't nothing. It is everything. And you need to ask your mother about that dream. Very. Soon."

Alexander suddenly wailed from one of the bedrooms. James turned to Marina and she forced a bright smile. "I'll be right back."

He watched her leave, wanting only to be with her right then, sharing in the joys of parenthood.

"Go," Kaye said to him with a little smile. "She needs you now."

James didn't need to be told twice. He followed the direction Marina had gone, and found her in a small bedroom with Rocco by the cot, as if on guard.

"Good boy," Marina praised Rocco, and the dog whined a little, as if telling her to hurry and stop the noise.

She picked up Alexander and snuggled him close. His cries intensified, and James saw Marina droop, clearly fatigued by the demands of motherhood and an infant who probably rarely slept. Little wonder she'd lost weight.

"Are you okay?" he asked.

She jumped at James' voice behind her, then slowly turned. And though she tried hard to look in control, she failed miserably. Her bottom lip wobbled as she insisted, "I'm fine."

James stepped forward. "Can I hold him for a bit?"

Marina nodded, relief tellingly etched into her hollowed face. James took him, his voice awed. "He's so big now.

Growing fast." His nose wrinkled. "I think he left a surprise in his nappy."

Marina nodded and said numbly, "I better change him."

"You look beat. How about I change him while you make him a bottle, or are you still breastfeeding?"

"Thanks. I am tired. Alexander—" She swept a hand towards her son. "—he doesn't sleep much. And, no, I bottle feed him now."

After James had changed Alexander, he picked up the hiccupping baby and settled him against a shoulder. Carrying the little bundle into the kitchen, something within him ached as he inhaled the baby and talcum powder scent.

He'd never before imagined himself as boyfriend or husband material, and least of all a father. But he was seeing with a clarity now that was startling. He hungered for the very things that'd never before tempted him.

Marina scooped formula into Alexander's bottle, though her attention seemed caught by her Aunt Kaye in the lounge room, who leaned over the tarot cards, her expression puzzled.

Marina tested the temperature of the milk on the inside of her wrist, when Kaye shook her head, murmuring, "That doesn't make sense. What is all the blood over his hands?"

James passed Alexander to Marina before he turned towards Kaye, the too-familiar feeling of dread and denial once again filling his gut. "Who has blood on their hands?"

Kaye gestured to the chair. "I think you should sit down, James. It appears your reading isn't quite finished."

He did as she'd asked. "So . . . what do the cards say?"

"There is a man close to you, James, a Taurus." Kaye frowned. "I can't get the image out of my head. H-he has blood dripping through his hands."

Marina sat on the lounge chair, feeding a now quiet Alexander his bottle. But her presence this once didn't ease the tautness in his shoulders.

"My sister accused my dad of having blood on his hands." He shook his head. "His birthday is in a couple of days."

A Taurus.

"Ah." Kaye collected her tarot cards and placed them carefully in their cloth, nodding to herself but revealing nothing more. "Well I'm sorry the reading couldn't have ended on a more positive note."

Alexander coughed and abruptly cried.

James stood and held his arms out for the infant. "May I?"

Marina nodded. "Of course."

He took the baby and bottle from Marina's hands and then popped the teat into Alexander's hungry mouth. James couldn't help but smile, tension leeching from his body at this simple act of feeding.

Marina sighed a little. "He likes you."

Kaye looked meaningfully at her niece. "You're in safe hands now."

Marina smiled, but James was aware of her pale, anxious face. Little wonder. Between his misunderstanding over her ex coming back into her life and the professor's death, it was little wonder her maternal instincts were falling apart.

Kaye stood. "Well, I'm already packed, and since the taxi has been booked and will be here soon, I guess this is goodbye."

Marina moved forward, giving her aunt a hug. "Thanks so much for all your help. I don't know what I would have done without you."

Aunt Kaye held her tight, before she stepped back. "It was a pleasure. If you ever need me, just give me a holler. I'm only a few hours away."

Alexander coughed and James tucked the bottle into his pocket before holding the baby against his shoulder once again, gently patting his back. "I think he's drifting off to sleep. Would you like me to put him back into his cot?" James asked quietly. He flashed Kaye a smile. "It was nice meeting you. I'm not sure what to make of the reading, but I thank you."

Kaye nodded. "It was nice to meet you, too. I'm glad you're here for my niece and her baby."

James left Marina to say her final goodbye to her aunt, just as the taxi driver pulled up outside and gave a toot from the driveway.

With Alexander asleep in his cot once more, James stepped back into the lounge room, where Marina stayed immobile in the opened front door. "I'm going to miss her," she said, turning to face him.

James took hold of her hands. "I'm here for you . . . if you want me to be."

Whatever resistance she'd clung onto dissolved right then. "I want," she breathed.

They moved together, his hands cupping her behind, her arms twining over his shoulders. When his mouth covered hers, she sighed surrender, as lost as he was to passion that had been too long denied. They belonged together. Always. James broke apart first, aware his willpower could only be stretched so far when it came to the beautiful Marina. Except when she looked up, he could see a yearning in her stare that would be mirrored in his own. "James, stay with me tonight?"

James pulled her back into his arms, something shifting inside his chest. "I'd like that." He grinned. "On one condition."

"Oh?"

"Have dinner with me first, I'll cook."

"But Alex—"

"Bring him. Or if he's asleep, I'm sure Josie wouldn't mind staying with him for a few hours, and will only be a phone call, or a shout, away."

She nodded. "When Josie comes to my house for her lessons, she always finds a way to spend time with him before she leaves. She's wonderful."

"Great. I'll talk to her, make sure she's happy to watch him, though I'm sure it won't be a problem."

He was more than confident of Josie's ability with Alexander. She wouldn't relapse. He could barely fathom how much better she was mentally and emotionally. Next thing he knew she'd be having male friends knocking at his door!

His sister was peeling and cutting potatoes in the kitchen when he walked back through his front door, whistling a tune. Striding into the kitchen, he asked, "Josie, will you—?"

"Yes, sure. Anything for you and Marina."

His logical mind instantly sifted through her preempted words. "So . . . you don't mind watching Alexander for Marina?"

She looked up, peeler in hand. "Not at all. And I'll take my pillow and stay in the spare room, that way you lovebirds can stay out as long as you like!" She nodded, thoughtfully adding, "Yes, that'll work out well."

"I don't think Marina expects that."

"Oh, she won't mind," Josie said airily. "We'll take care of everything."

He raised a brow. "We? You haven't been seeing Molly again, have you?"

"No. I've felt her near a few times, even heard her indistinctly. But I haven't seen her." Her smile was knowing and a little secretive. "She'll be there for us when the time comes."

Some three hours later, Alexander fed and burped, Josie tucked him into his cot. "Such a beautiful boy," she whispered.

Shame the real father was a lost cause.

She pulled the blanket up over his tiny shoulders. "Don't worry. We'll protect you."

Double-checking the window was locked tight, Josie called in Rocco, who immediately lay beside the cot, head on his paws.

Josie swallowed past her fear of dogs, or more to the point, her golden retriever phobia she'd suffered with ever since Maxwell's death. Step-by-step, she was overcoming her fears, her guilt, though everything inside her now screamed, *Retreat!*

She bent, managing a single stroke over the dog's silky, furred head. "Good boy, Maxwell." She jerked upright, and, swallowing convulsively, she corrected, "Rocco."

It may be too late for Maxwell, but she wouldn't be making the same mistake twice.

Alexander . . . now he, she could help.

"Stay, Rocco," she commanded, before pulling the door half shut behind her.

She'd left her poetry book on the kitchen table. She returned, opening it to a specific page. Using salt and pepper shakers as paper weights at each end, she then lit a candle on the table, ensuring its light pooled over the writing.

Satisfied, she moved silently into the spare bedroom, flicking off the lights as she went.

Marina leaned back in her chair, sighing with contentment. "Thanks for dinner, James. If I'd known you could cook so well, I'd have invited myself over much sooner."

James grinned, his eyes glinting in the candlelight. "I would have asked you—"

"—But I all but told you to stay away." She shrugged. "I'm only glad we both believe in second chances."

He leaned across the table, his breath warm as his mouth captured hers, his spicy scent wrapping around her senses and tugging her into his intoxicating vortex.

When he eased back, she slumped in her seat, breathless even as her heart beat a wild tattoo. She cleared her throat, getting onto her feet and gathering the dishes before putting them on the sink.

James' chair scraped backward, his tread headed her way. When he folded his arms around her, his warmth cocooning her body, she leaned against him, delighting in how her body slotted so naturally into his.

"The lights are out at your house," he murmured. "Alexander must be fast asleep."

Guilt gnawed in her belly. She'd been so caught up in the moment . . . in James. "I hadn't even noticed," she admitted starkly.

James turned her around, his eyes holding hers. "Are you okay?"

She nodded, swallowing back a sudden need to tell him that she was barely coping with motherhood. "Yes. Sure." Her laugh sounded forced. "Of course."

He frowned a little. "Josie has a way with babies. Always has, despite her mental history."

It was Marina's turn to frown. "I don't hold that against her, James, and I would never leave Alexander with someone I didn't think fit for the role."

"Josie is at peace with herself now," James allowed. "There won't be any going back to the hell she was at."

Marina nodded, and then went to turn back to the sink. "You cooked, I'll clean."

Suddenly his hands were on her forearms. "The dishes can wait," he said huskily. He turned her around, his eyes snaring hers. "There's something I've been wanting to show you."

"Oh?" she squeaked.

He slipped a hand into his pocket and pulled out a velvet box. With shaky hands she covered her mouth, withholding a squeal of pure joy. He sank onto one knee and opened the lid, revealing a beautiful princess-cut diamond ring.

"Marry me, Marina."

She looked into his brilliant gaze that glinted brighter than any diamond. All doubts vanished, washed away like sands in a relentless, inescapable tide.

"I-I, yes. Of course! Yes!"

He slipped the ring free and slid it up her finger. "You're my world, my light, my air, my everything," he said huskily. "I knew that even before the falls, before the birth of Alexander. I love you."

Her heart welled with an adoration that filled her eyes with tears. "I love you, too."

Desire shimmered like something delicious and decedent inside her womb when she whispered, "Take me, James. Make me yours."

He swept her into his arms and carried her effortlessly out of the kitchen and into his bedroom.

On a scrolled shelf above a wall mirror, he used his free hand to light a squat candle before closing the bedroom door behind them . . . closing them from the world.

There was something wholly intimate to the way he helped unbutton her dress and let it slide from her shoulders until it lay in a puddle at her feet.

Standing in her bra and lacy panties, her body still showing signs of her post pregnancy, she felt only pride as his stare moved down her like a caress, and back up again.

She moved close, and as his fingertips traced the contours of her breasts, the indent of her waist, she closed her eyes, allowing the sensation of his touch to wash over her.

His fingers glided low. She let out a breathless "oh" when he hooked his thumbs inside her panties and tugged downward. Her eyelids flicking open, she stepped out of the miniscule piece of lace and then turned around.

He unclipped her bra with deft hands that shook slightly. His dark stare glittered when she swung back to face him, his expression openly adoring.

"So beautiful," he whispered.

She'd never thought herself remotely beautiful, not after so many years of Roger's taunts, but just then she truly believed she was.

The certainty unleashed something fierce and wanton inside, a boldness that saw her step forward and unbutton his shirt. She dragged it over his shoulders and down his arms before tossing it aside. Crouching low, she unzipped his trousers, pushing them and his boxer briefs down past the jutting hardness of his arousal, his strong thighs and muscled calves.

He helped discard his footwear before she moved back up, pressing kisses along his taut belly, his lightly haired chest, and the puckered ridges of his nipples.

His expression was pure tenderness in the flickering light. And just then she knew everything was going to be okay—more than okay. She loved this man with every breath, with every heartbeat she had.

Moving up onto her toes, she claimed his mouth with her own, pouring her love into the kiss, her soul.

James drew her closer still, deepening the kiss that had his heart squeeze tight with emotion, his resolve about their future one hundred percent certain.

Marina was the only woman for him.

James dragged in a breath, so hungry with love for this woman.

"James, make love to me."

He would give her the world, if she asked.

Leading her to his bed, she lay down on the mattress, waiting expectantly, her eyes soft and yet beckoning. James caught a faint whiff of her lilac scent, and then his body was covering hers, her legs tangling behind his hips and urging his possession.

His pulse skipped a beat as he paused, then pushed deep inside, her inner warmth sheathing him, a perfect fit. They began to move to the beautiful, sacred rhythm of lovers, rocking and undulating as one, her skin sliding softer than satin beneath his.

Her eyes glistened. "I love you," she whispered.

Something inside him melted. "I love you, too."

Then all thought left his mind, their lovemaking taking him to whole new realm, where time ceased to matter, ceased to exist.

Marina abruptly gasped, holding him close as she shuddered beneath him, around him, her clenched inner muscles holding him deep.

He groaned with his own release, swept away by the magic, the sheer wonder of their joining. And the utter belief and acceptance he'd found his soul mate.

*

Roger swayed, his eyes gritty and burning with fatigue. Already his body screamed for a shot, a hit straight into the veins that would take him to paradise.

After two days straight without sleep, wired on drugs and thoughts of Marina and his baby, his boy, he knew stalking, spying and scaring his ex from a distance was no longer enough.

Marina and the baby had become an obsession even worse than the drugs drying up his veins.

Seeing her with that doctor, the neighbor, had caused something inside him to snap and decay.

He squinted at Marina's house once again. It was past time to teach her a lesson! The lights had gone out a few hours before, and now all was quiet.

Now or never.

He had a fair idea where the baby's room was situated. He tried the window, cursing under his breath. It wouldn't budge. Locked tight.

Crouching in the shadows of a gum tree, he pulled out a knife and cut slowly, methodically through the lounge room window's fly screen.

He could only hope Rocco, the mongrel dog who had never liked him, wouldn't wake and give him away.

A single candle burned on the table of an otherwise eerily dark house. The hairs on the back of his neck stood up. Something wasn't quite right. Still he kept on, adrenaline for now keeping thoughts of drugs at bay.

Knife still in hand, he paused at the table, squinting at the book spread open. "What the hell?" he muttered. He peered harder and read the handwriting at the top of a passage of poetry. "Karma."

His senses prickled wildly and he spun, knife raised, his heart jagged in his throat. No one there! Sweat dripped from his brow as a round of shivers sent prickles of goose-bumps across his skin.

He straightened, looking around and swallowing convulsively. "This ain't right." But he couldn't leave, not yet, not without knowing for sure he wasn't going insane . . . not without his prize.

He swiped a forearm across his brow. Damn it! Marina was making him paranoid!

He turned back, his eyes drawn to the words on the page.

Hey there, you, with the incredulous grin

Hiding 'neath your skin, withering within.

Did you really think there'd be no cross to bear?

So what? You didn't care? Has nothing . . . no one, ever made you feel?

This life, the next . . . it's all too real.

No good peering back, at the past you left behind,

Waiting for someone, you'll never find.

Your time has arrived, the moment is now.

Karma is here. You've been found.

~Kylie Sheaffe & Mel Teshco

Roger took a step back, his skin crawling. The words seemed almost to taunt him, to play with his mind.

At the suddenly overpowering and unmistakable sensation of someone watching him, he jerked his head up. He took another step back, his eyes going wide.

Oh, shit!

"I know you," he whispered.

Chills slid up and down his spine. It was the neighbor's sister, and yet it wasn't. She was there, but someone else was there, too. Right beside the girl with accusation flashing from her blue eyes was a white, shadowy outline, a duplicate.

The duplicate turned and moved away, flowing like smoke on a gentle breeze before stilling beside the bare dining room wall. His heart jumped, but his legs were weighted, too heavy to move.

The . . . thing lifted a fuzzy arm. One pointed finger touched the wall. And suddenly, a bright red letter formed like a splash of crimson against the white wall. Four more letters revealed the word karma, an accusation that caused his blood to run cold.

He swayed, a rush of dizziness assailing him.

Just breathe.

The girl pointed at him, and then the wall, her eerie voice filling the silence. "Your days are numbered."

His pulse jackknifed, and then beat out-of-control as the duplicate figure began writing random numbers all over the once blank wall.

He shook his head, slowly at first, then wildly. "No. No . . . no, please! I never meant for anything bad to happen. I never wanted to hurt anyone."

The girl stepped forward. "And yet your zipper scar gives you away." Her blue eyes narrowed. "We know what you did. We saw you. *Murderer.*"

"No. No, please! I shouldn't have driven. I know that now. I didn't mean to hit him. I was high as a kite—"

The girl closed her eyes, her voice loud and clear. "Two-twenty-three on the day they were wed, blue paint splattered red. James Edward . . . dead."

He stumbled backward then, away from the girl and her duplicate, away from the writing on the wall. He tripped, thudding onto the floor. "Make it stop, make this nightmare stop!"

A baby began to wail . . . his baby.

He drew his knees up and pushed his face into his crossed arms. "What am I doing? What have I done?"

Chapter Five

Marina woke with a start, automatically peering at the digital clock on James' side table.

Ten past nine. They'd been asleep less than an hour.

A cell phone abruptly chimed somewhere inside the house.

Something was wrong. Very wrong. She didn't know how she knew, but somehow she did.

James stirred as she disentangled from his arms. She threw on his striped robe hanging from the inner door handle and all but sprinted to the phone on the kitchen bench.

Josie's voice snapped her wide-awake. "You might want to come home."

"What?"

Blue and red lights were flashing just outside the windows. In her driveway. The cell phone dropped from her grasp. Her heart crashed to a standstill.

For a moment, she swayed, light-headed. Then found the strength to retrace her steps. "James!" Was that half-strangled croak her voice?

James jackknifed out of bed, hopping on one foot then the other to pull on a pair of boxers.

"Something's wrong! I've got to go home." Marina forced her legs to carry her to the front door.

James caught up to her. His hand interlacing with hers gave her strength. Terror squeezed her chest as they broke into a sprint.

Oh, God, please let Alexander be okay.

A police officer stepped towards them. "Please, stay back, we're questioning a suspect inside."

Marina pushed past, snapping, "This is my house. My baby is inside."

She stilled on a horrified gasp. "Roger!"

Two policemen pushed the handcuffed man through the front door and down the steps, and as he staggered past, his eyes wild, he shouted, "That woman inside is a witch, a witch! Take a look, the writing's on the wall!" He hung his head, shoulders slumping as he whimpered, "I never meant to kill him, it was an accident."

"Oh my God!" She threw James a terrified look, aware the blood had all but drained from her face. "Alexander."

James half-carried her inside, but they stilled at the sight of Josie standing in the kitchen, serene and at peace as she fed Alexander his bottle.

A police officer followed James and Marina. Clearing his throat, he said, "Ah, Marina, is it?"

She didn't turn, couldn't take her eyes off her son. The maternal instincts she'd kept locked away had burst free, flooding her heart, her soul, with love. Terrible that it had taken this, for her to wake up to the truth.

She nodded abstractedly. "Yes."

"We'll need to take a statement from you down at the station." She twisted to face the young officer and he smiled reassurance. "Just routine, nothing to worry about."

James' brow furrowed with concern. "I'll go with you."

Marina shook her head. "No, I'd much prefer you stay with Alexander after everything that's happened."

Don't let anything happen to him.

"Of course." He smiled reassurance, the love shining from his eyes unmistakable. "I'll be waiting for you," he murmured.

*

Robyn sat at the table in the semi-darkness, staring at her hands . . . at her wedding ring she couldn't bear to take off her finger.

It'd been almost a month and a half since her husband's funeral. And still, she hadn't moved on. Not one bit.

The clock ticked, but she cared little about time. A car droned past outside where, in the real world, people laughed, people loved, people . . . lived.

The phone rang . . . and rang. Eventually the answering machine clicked on. She ignored the message. It was late to be making a phone call. Maybe it was something important, something urgent?

She stayed put, unable to rouse herself enough to care. Her hands cradled her belly even as guilt and self-doubt soured the love for the baby growing in her womb.

Her dream of being a Mom had become a nightmare, like ashes in her mouth.

For so long she'd been consumed by the limbo of infertility and the shattered hopes of three miscarriages. She'd had to either accept life without the joy of motherhood or continue on in the fight for her heart's greatest desire. And now . . . now that she was pregnant, she felt empty. Barren. Her life a brushstroke of black and white.

For the sake of her baby she had to break out of this rut of despair.

She couldn't.

A recent visit to her GP had almost seen her put into hospital. With her skyrocketing blood pressure, her age, and obvious weight loss, she'd only just managed to talk him out of the idea.

She'd promised to eat well, to get more sleep.

Robyn sighed. She'd never broken a promise before.

This morning when she'd discovered spots of blood on her briefs, an all-too-familiar rush of fear had all but disabled her.

A tear ran down her cheek, and another. She got to her feet, swaying with dizzy lightheadedness. At least by living in ignorance she hadn't had to face reality.

But perhaps it was time to talk to someone. If she didn't, she'd go mad.

Picking up the phone, she dialed James' mobile.

A young woman answered, and Robyn frowned distractedly when she realized it wasn't Marina. "Hello." Her voice cracked and she winced. She sounded so ancient. She swallowed, moistening her throat. "Can I speak to James, please?"

"I'm sorry, he's not home. But I can pass him a message if you like?"

"I . . . I don't think so." She started to shake. Fresh tears threatened to spill.

A pause, and from the other end of the line, the young woman said, "I'm Josie, James' sister."

She sounded lovely, so grounded and normal. Just listening to her voice made everything almost bearable. It was like taking hold of a life raft just before going under.

Josie's voice gentled. "Is everything alright?" A pause, then, "It isn't, is it?"

Robyn suddenly recollected Marina's words. You'd love Josie. She's an angel. And in that moment, Robyn could well believe it. A wave of peace, of relief washed over her even before Josie added, "You need someone to talk to, don't you? I can feel that by your sadness."

Robyn nodded, her throat thick. Fool. It wasn't like Josie could see her!

Static whispered across the line, as if Josie had moved a little before she said, "Robyn, I'm more than happy to come over."

Robyn's throat closed over completely. She couldn't answer, couldn't talk. Tears threatened again. This stranger was willing to come and share her pain, and damned if she wasn't desperate now for some company.

"I'll get the address from my brother. Expect me within half an hour, okay?"

Robyn managed to make some barely audible sound, and then hang up. And for the first time since her husband's death, she felt just a little lighter.

Only then every tick of the clock seemed interminable, every second, every minute an endless march . . .

Headlights flashed momentarily across her dark walls. She moved unsteadily to the front door and swung it open. James' sister climbed out of a taxi then traversed the wide, cobblestone driveway, a book tucked under her arm and clasping what looked like a casserole dish wrapped in a tea towel.

Josie smiled. "Hi, Robyn. James sent his apologies, but he had to stay with Marina's son while she's . . . otherwise engaged."

"Hi, Josie. Of course." She managed a smile that for once wasn't forced. "Come in. And thank you for dropping everything for me at such a late hour."

Josie climbed the round of large steps and followed her inside. She gestured at the casserole dish. "Marina and James had lots of leftovers. I thought you might like some?"

Even cold, the rich aromas filled the air, and Robyn registered the spiced scent of gravy, steak, and vegetables. She nodded, aware just how weak she'd let herself become by an almost nonexistent appetite. "Thank you. Actually I'm ravenous."

As Josie set down the large book and then preoccupied herself by sliding the casserole dish into the oven, Robyn hesitantly asked, "Do you . . . do you believe in life after death?"

Josie pushed the oven door closed, then turned to her with a gentle smile. This clearly wasn't a sensitive topic. "Yes. Yes, I do. I believe your husband is on a higher plane now, but he keeps watch."

"You really think so?" she breathed, wishing so fervently Josie was right it was like a painful, deep-rooted ache in her heart.

Josie nodded, her young stare so worldly-wise. "The true love that you shared is too strong a bond to be broken, even in the afterlife."

Robyn closed her eyes on a sigh. "There have been a few times—well, more than a few—when I imagined his presence around me." She opened her eyes. "I wondered and hoped. But thought I was just being silly."

"Never silly, no."

"So you believe he's watching me now?"

"Yes. He sees you. He knows you still need him. And he awaits the birth of his son."

"Our son?"

"Yes. I, ah, I don't usually speak about certain things, but I hear and see stuff most people don't."

Robyn spread her hands across her stomach, abstractedly aware even at twelve weeks along her stomach was almost flat. "I'm not sure what I believe now. I'm not sure it even counts anymore."

"Robyn—"

"Look, I'm . . . I'm not sure if my baby is even alive, let alone if it's a boy or girl. I've already lost three babies early in my pregnancy . . . and I've . . . I've been bleeding on and off for weeks now. We'd stopped IVF and it never occurred to me until too late . . . if I'd known, perhaps my James would have known, too."

"Perhaps he had a bit of an idea," Josie suggested softly.

Robyn shook her head, rejecting the idea even as a seed of hope bloomed within. "The bleeding is like a nightmare repeating itself, only this time it's worse. This time I'm all alone and I'm too scared to bond with my baby when the chances are—"

Josie shook her head. "The stronger the bond, the harder your baby will fight." She moved forward, placing her hands over Robyn's. "And believe me, your baby isn't going anywhere. He is a fighter."

Robyn bent her head and croaked, "I'll hold on to that hope with everything I have." She dragged in a shaky breath. "I only wish my husband wasn't taken from me, wish our baby could still have two parents."

"I know you do," Josie whispered. "And though I can't expect you to believe me, just know that the man responsible for your husband's death is being brought to justice."

"The man responsible. How did you—?"

"He is Marina's ex-husband and the father to Alexander. Long story short, he confessed to his crime. He'll have no choice but to serve his time."

Marina's ex-husband? Oh, dear lord. Robyn fought to make sense of it all. But there was no sense to be made of such a senseless act. Bitter grief stirred within. "Nothing will ever bring my husband back."

Josie bent low, her voice soothing. "I know. And though it's probably no consolation right now, I really believe each one of us has to pay our dues, whether in this lifetime or the next."

Robyn sighed. "I hope you're right."

Josie smiled. "I truly believe I am." She straightened, and then turned away from her to scrunch her eyes at something—no, nothing—at the other side of the room. In-between intermittent nods, she said, "But now you . . . you have something to fight for . . . your baby . . . your husband's baby. You must . . . keep the faith."

Robyn shivered, goose-bumps erupting over her skin. Keep the faith. It had been a phrase her husband had used many times in their mission to become parents. "You're right." My husband is right. "I lost sight of what is important."

Josie smiled. Then turned and retrieved the book she'd left on the kitchen counter. "Whenever I was down, my brother would read me a poem from this book he bought for my birthday. I'd love to share one with you?"

Robyn knew no poem would heal the world of hurt inside. But it was a thoughtful gesture, all the same. "Thank you, yes."

Josie nodded, then opened a seemingly random page and began to read.

No pain, no sorrow, no despair—

I never expected to feel in such a way
Elation, peace, and utter bliss, it's my air,
A reward after my earthly stay.
The view from here's astounding
The colors light my way
No map, no idea, it's confounding
But I know my place; I can no longer stay
Physically departed, my energy lives on
In the highest loving vibration
The past, the present, and beyond—
Our love, forever in preservation . . .
Till the day when, again, together we are one."
~Mel Teshco & Kylie Sheaffe

Robyn didn't realize she was crying until Josie set the book aside and pulled free a couple of tissues from the box on a nearby occasional table.

"Thank you." Robyn swiped at her nose and blotted the moisture from her face. "That was beautiful. It . . . it really moved me."

"You're welcome. And I'm so glad it touched you."

Robyn sniffled. "I only wish you could have met my James. He was a wonderful man."

Josie returned to the oven and retrieved the hot casserole dish from inside. She busied herself spooning most of the stew into a bowl before placing it onto the table and waiting for her to sit and eat.

Robyn felt like a recalcitrant child as she sat and took a mouthful. She closed her eyes, sighing as the meat melted in her mouth, the flavor bursting on her tongue, reanimating her taste buds.

Josie took the chair beside her. "Actually I did get to meet him. And I agree. He really was an extraordinary man."

Robyn placed the spoon into the bowl. "That's odd. My husband never mentioned meeting you."

Josie focused on her clasped hands, as though choosing her words carefully. "It was a rather unconventional meeting." She paused. "In a dream, I sat beside him in his car just before it crashed."

By the time Josie paid the taxi fare and slipped inside James' house, it was a little over an hour after midnight.

But she was restless, not anywhere near ready to sleep just yet. Since her 'recovery' she'd had to come to terms with a lot of things in her life. A lot of emotional baggage to put to rest.

And she'd done that. Mostly.

Seeing Marina at the depths of her despair had made her realize if she wanted to be completely free of her demons, to move on with her life, she had to face her biggest fears.

Withholding a shudder, she squared her shoulders and walked into her bedroom, towards her old dresser. Opening the top drawer, she retrieved the square cardboard box inside. It held her most precious mementos.

With shaky hands she lifted the lid, ignoring everything but the old silver chain. Maxwell's dog collar.

She lifted it out, letting each heavy link slide through her fingers. Funny, now she had the collar in her hand, the fear seemed to fade away, like it had never been.

The hairs on the back of her neck prickled, a whisper cool breath of air sliding across her skin. Molly? Her throat convulsed and her vision distorted. "I'm not bad," she said. "I'm not bad."

In that short moment, relief flooded her system, permeated to the very marrow of her bones. A soul-touching self-forgiveness that left her trembling with stark joy.

And then she was alone again.

She let out a shaky breath. Now . . . now it was time to say goodbye. Time to let Maxwell go. She'd been selfish keeping him from crossing over all these years, but guilt had powered a childish need to keep him with her—if only in spirit.

"Josie, you're home."

She jumped, turning to see a bleary-eyed James in the doorway. "Yes, I got back a few minutes ago. But I-I couldn't sleep."

He blew out a weary breath. "I know what you mean. It's been a big day. Too much to take in really."

He propped a shoulder on the doorframe, staring into space as though deep in thought. "Marina told me everything. To be honest, I can hardly fathom it was Marina's ex who killed the professor." He shook his head and turned to face her, all seriousness now. "But you knew that, didn't you, Josie? Knew Roger was the killer?"

She sighed. "Not at first." A round of shivers had her skin prickle with goose-bumps as Roger's ugly zipper scar filled her mind. "But later, yes. Yes, I did. I guess it's just another thread in the complex tapestry of my dreams." She lifted her chin, echoing, "But you know that, don't you, James?"

He swiped a hand over his face. "Yes, I guess I do, I just—"

She frowned at the shocked dismay on his face. "James, what's the matter?"

"Where did you get that dog collar?"

She held it up. "This?" She let out a breath. "It was Maxwell's. I wanted something to remind me of him . . . remind me of my sin."

"It wasn't Rocco at all," he whispered starkly. "It was Maxwell I saw." He stared at her. "But he wasn't with you, was he, Josie?"

She slid the collar back into the box, a sudden knowing filling her from the inside out. "I think you might have met Molly."

Chapter Six

Carlton, Australia

Sunday, April 24th

James lay on his bed with his hands curled behind his head, his eyes wide open in the utter darkness. With the curtains closed tight, only the faint digital display on his alarm clock cast any light. For possibly the hundredth time, he read the clock, 3:12 a.m. and yet he couldn't sleep.

Neither, apparently, could his sister.

Josie played her violin from her bedroom at the other side of the house, the haunting notes washing over him in beautiful harmony, even as he drowned in a sea of his own deep thoughts.

Marina had come back from the police station and insisted he go home to his sister. She'd wanted to ensure Josie was okay after the confrontation with Roger.

James had been torn, agreeing only after Marina had explained they'd have the rest of their lives together.

Josie played the instrument until it soared, then dipped into a couple of lower notes that were somehow achingly moving. In the silence, his lips pulled into a half-smile. It seemed his little sister had finally exhausted herself.

He rolled onto his side, registering the sudden waves of weariness descending over him.

No doubt the Bowheart children would be in fine form for their father's birthday dinner tomorrow night.

With a sigh, he closed his eyes, succumbing to the darkness that immediately engulfed him.

A dry stick snapped beneath one of his polished shoes. James peered around him, a little anxious. Damn, it was so dark! Was he lost? He loosened the knot of his silk tie, suddenly sticky and hot . . . and overdressed.

He'd been on duty and traversing the hospital corridor, hadn't he? His brow scrunched. He couldn't seem to remember.

He shivered, only just making out the dim, silvery outline of tree trunks. Branches swayed, their leaves rustling ever so quietly in the breeze.

Everything was normal . . .

Something, a warning edged his consciousness, a trickle of unease moving down his spine.

"James!"

Josie? It sounded like her, but there was an echo. Two voices had called out simultaneously from somewhere ahead.

He moved forward, but the ground beneath sucked at his feet, pulling him downward, slowing him, sapping his strength until will alone kept him going.

"James!"

He was closer now. Much closer. He lunged forward, his feet squelching from the bog as he pushed up onto the exposed, lumpy root of a huge fig tree. A sudden wind had the branches pitching above as he gripped the gnarled trunk. He peered around.

And saw them.

He sucked in a sharp breath.

Two flames hovered just above the bare ground, burning side-by-side, blazing red-orange and bright.

Impossible! He swayed for a moment, trying to gather his thoughts. But nothing rational formed, nothing logical at all. He moved forward, careless now of the quagmire beneath his feet.

His skin broke out in sweat as he approached the flames that were in the shape of a person . . . two people. Two women. He sucked in another breath, hot air parching his throat and lungs. He shook his head in denial, though the proof was there to see. The flames were taking on distinct features, becoming human.

"Josie?" he rasped.

Yes. They were both Josie, he could see that now. And yet, they were not. One of the flames sputtered, dying out. He staggered forward, inexplicable fear sending his pulse racing. "What's happening? Please, don't go!"

The other human torch, roaring bright and beautiful, flowed sideward, merging with the weaker flame. For one millisecond—forever?—nothing happened.

His senses screamed, seconds before the lava hot explosion flung him backward like a matchstick in a hurricane. Seconds later, sprawled helplessly in the cold, wet mud, he forced his head up, mesmerized by the beautiful inferno.

The lone figure of Josie reached out from the flames, beckoning to him now like the warmth of a fireplace on a frosty winter's night. "James. Can't you see? I'm okay now. I'm whole."

An alarm abruptly reverberated. She held his stare for an infinitesimal beat, her eyes growing wide. Then an invisible force reeled him backward at ground blurring, phenomenal speed.

James jerked upright, his mind racing. He dripped with sweat, his heart bouncing out from his chest.

"Some dream," he muttered hoarsely. He hadn't had one like that since he'd used drugs.

He ran a hand over his eyes, releasing an unsteady breath. Since his lifestyle change, he'd been waking up refreshed, healthy. Yet, right then it actually seemed plausible he'd walked every single step in his dream.

"Shit!" He jumped back, his pulse thundering in his ears. He swallowed rebuke. "Josie."

In her white nightgown, with her silver hair falling down past her shoulders, and her beautiful eyes red-rimmed from lack of sleep . . . she was the epitome of his dream.

He shook his head. "You scared me half to death!"

"Sorry, James." She held out his cell phone. "But you didn't answer. It's for you."

So that was the alarm that'd invaded his subconscious and entered his dream! He reached out, claiming the cell phone. He swallowed. "Thanks," he said to Josie, all but dismissing her.

He was in no mood right then for niceties. Not even for his little sister. She disappeared through his bedroom door as he muttered, "Hello."

"James. It's me."

He scowled. "Tom?"

"Yeah." A pause. "I haven't seen you at the hospital or the club lately?"

"I know." He sighed. "The truth is, after the professor's death I had a lot of soul searching to do." He gripped the phone, rubbing at his temple. "But that's not why you called, is it?"

Tom's laugh was strained. "You know me too well."

"I guess I do." He exhaled heavily. "It's not like you to beat around the bush. What's wrong?"

"I'm . . . I'm in trouble, mate."

Any lingering tiredness evaporated, along with thoughts of the weird dream. He swung his legs to the side of the bed, spine taut. "What do you mean? What happened?"

"A drug deal went bad. I was with Stevie." His voice broke. "Two men pulled a knife on us, man, threatened Stevie. What was I supposed to do? I couldn't just stand back and let them get away with it."

This wasn't the cocky, brazen Tom he knew. This was a new Tom, scared witless and unashamedly sorry for himself.

"Tom, what did you do?"

"I fought for her life, James, what else was I to do? I got the knife, and, well, one of them died."

James closed his eyes, Tom's words coming back to haunt him. You owe me one. "Shit, Tom. You killed him? Shit!" He rubbed the throbbing behind his temple a little harder, knowing exactly what was coming next.

Right on cue, Tom's voice broke the silence. "Yes, I did! And now I need to you talk to your dad for me. If anyone can play dirty and get me off, it's him."

Tom wanted more than a favor. He wanted a 'get out of jail free card'.

"Look, I'm seeing my dad later tonight. I'll ask him if he'll represent you. But I can't make any promises. I'm not exactly in his good books right now."

Tom's sigh down the line was loud and clear. "I'm counting on you, James."

When the connection went dead, he pushed onto his feet and pulled open the blinds. Afternoon sunlight streamed through, blinding him. He'd slept half the day away.

He had a lot to do before his dad's birthday dinner tonight. But first a shower. And then a visit to his lovely neighbor.

Marina's smile as she opened the door to his knock some half an hour later, said it all. She radiated happiness and beamed with positive energy.

"James!" She swept the door wider still, moving aside to let him inside. And he couldn't help but notice with pride the ring on her finger, flashing in the afternoon sun. "I've just put Alexander down for his nap. Come in!"

He stepped towards her and clasped her face gently in his hands, kissing her lips until they softened and responded under his. When he finally drew back, he voiced, "I missed you."

Delight shone in her stare even as she exclaimed, "It's only been one night!"

"Yes. And quite possibly the longest night of my life."

Her lips twitched. "I'm sorry to hear that."

"You look anything but sorry," he said with a wry grin.

She smiled. "You're right. Actually, I'm flattered a hot young doctor is losing sleep over me." She clasped his hands. "But I'm guessing you didn't come here to tell me that?"

He nodded. "Do you remember me mentioning my dad's upcoming birthday?"

"Ah, yes, when my aunt did your reading. The Taurus man."

"Yes. Well it's today actually. And the Bowheart family always get together for a special birthday dinner." He squeezed her hands a little. "It's short notice, but I-I wanted to know if you wanted to come. My parents aren't exactly the loving—"

"Yes."

"Great. Fantastic." He felt flustered suddenly.

What would Marina think of his Mom and dad? Would they pretend to be great parents and act 'normal' or would everything be blown out of proportion like it was their last dinner together?

They hadn't yet seen Josie's recovery, probably thought it was too good to be true. He swallowed, imagining Josie entering the Bowheart lion's den. Would taking his sister there be detrimental to her health?

He swiped a thumb back and forth across the soft skin of Marina's hand. "Just promise you won't take anything they say personally."

"I promise, James." Her smile shone from her stare. "Whatever they do or say in no way reflects how I feel for you."

His heart overflowed with love for her, so much so he was unable to form the words to tell her before she became all business and practical-minded, evidently oblivious to his thoughts.

"I will probably have to leave early though if that's okay. Alexander is already in a routine now, and I'm starting student music lessons from tomorrow again."

James nodded, the tension ebbing. Marina was definitely feeling safe now if she'd organized her work commitments, once again doing what she loved.

It was past time he got his life back in order too. He had his university studies to resume and medical rounds at hospital to attend. His mind whirled. Graduation was just around the corner! He cleared his throat, willing calm. "Of course. I'll make sure you're home early."

No doubt the dinner would spiral into a disaster anyway. The earlier they left, the better. "I'll let my parents know to expect one more guest." He flicked a look at his watch. "How about we leave in a couple of hours?"

"Sure. I'll be ready."

A few hours later, James swallowed trepidation as he pulled his car into the granite driveway of the Bowheart residence.

He'd been concerned for his sister, but was Marina ready for this? He probably should have prepared her somehow, explained what may well happen.

Marina retrieved the nappy bag as he unclipped Alexander from his baby seat and cradled him close.

He glanced at Josie. She'd been ecstatic with the news of his engagement to Marina. Shame her huge smile had slowly disappeared the closer they got to their parents' house. With her poetry book in hand, she appeared serene, but he had to wonder just what was going on inside her head.

Too late to back out now.

His austere mother waited at the opened doors as they approached. At the sight of the baby in his arms, his mother's look of utter horror, though quickly masked, was almost comical.

"James," his mother greeted. "Thank you for coming." Her mouth pinched tighter still. "And a baby, too?"

He smiled. "Yes, Mother. I'd like you to meet my son, Alexander." At her hiss of disbelief, he tucked his free arm around Marina and announced, "And my fiancée, Marina."

"Fiancée?" His mother's horrified stare swung to Marina and to the engagement ring. She turned back to her son. "But why? When did this happen? And a baby?" She shook her head. "He's not yours. No! There's not one drop of Bowheart blood in his veins."

He frowned. He'd expected a little tension, but this? She was almost hysterical. "Mother—"

"We'll pay for a paternity test," his mother continued in a high-pitched tone, her good breeding and manners seemingly forgotten this once. "You'll not be roped into a marriage by some scheming little—"

"I'm pleased to meet you, too, Mrs. Bowheart," Marina injected with a raised brow. "And, no, James isn't the father. As a matter-of-fact, the real father to Alexander is behind bars right now."

As his mother stood gaping like a fish on a hot rock, Josie abruptly giggled.

James frowned at her, and then swung a look at Marina. She visibly curbed anything beyond a smile. But suddenly he was laughing right along with his sister, feeling less like a Bowheart and more himself than he ever had before.

He'd never felt more carefree. And neither, apparently, had Josie.

His little sister would be fine.

His mother snapped her head around, focused now on her daughter. "Jocelyn, I hope you have no plans this time to ruin our family dinner?"

Josie's giggles subsided. Her chin tilted. "Hello, Mother. I'm good, thank you," she added pointedly.

Their dad appeared in the doorway beside his wife. And though they stood side-by-side, James realized just how disconnected his parents really were.

I've never been in love before, never had a true and meaningful relationship to compare theirs with.

He nodded. "Happy Birthday, Dad." He pulled the small, wrapped present from out of his jacket pocket. "This is from all of us."

The platinum Cartier pen probably wouldn't be received graciously, regardless of thought or expense.

His father took the gift without comment. Then, eyeing Alexander, he said, "Please tell me that baby isn't part of my birthday present!"

James snuggled Alexander close, smiling down at the little cherub who slept soundly in his arms. "No way. Nobody will be taking this little guy from us."

At his mother's audible gasp he looked up with a frown. "He might not be my flesh and blood, Mom, but I love him like he's my own son."

"What are you saying?" his dad demanded, looking at him as if he'd finally lost his mind.

His mother's voice came out like ice. "He's marrying that woman. He's taking on a readymade family."

A frog chirped into the silence. Then his dad's face creased into a grin. He stepped forward and put a hand on his shoulder. "Well good for you, son! Looks like you've found a lovely, warm woman to cuddle at night. Unlike the cold—"

"Dad, please. That's enough," James warned. Yes, his mother was a cold wife, a cold person. But it didn't give any right for his dad to expose her flaws to the world. Heaven only knew his dad had more than enough flaws of his own. "You've been drinking again, haven't you?"

He spread his hands expansively. "Surely you don't begrudge your old man a couple of scotches on his own birthday?"

"It's been more than a couple, and you know it,"

Margaret hissed. Squaring her shoulders, she stepped aside. "I guess you all should come in."

Despite his mother's usual display of detachment, James noted the fissures in her armor, perceived much of the steel in her spine was crumbling under the strain.

His mother led the group towards the formal living room, where creaky, barely used black leather recliners waited.

His dad brought up the rear, saying loudly to Josie, "You really do look well now, my dear. I guess that means no more silly talk and speaking of blood on my hands, hmm?"

"I guess not," Josie replied neutrally.

As everyone took a seat, Marina took Alexander from his arms, before taking a recliner next to his mother who was perched primly of the edge of her seat.

His dad seemed entranced by the book in Josie's hand. "What have you got there?"

Josie swept a hand over the plain leather cover with its gold embossed lettering. "It's a poetry book, Dad. I thought you might like me to read one to you later."

"Don't waste your time. Poetry doesn't interest me. You should know that."

She held his gaze. "I think these verses will strike a chord."

"If you say so," he all but sneered.

Alexander began to fuss, impatient little hungry cries that would only increase in volume. Marina looked over to James. "I better go and make him a bottle."

When he shifted forward in his seat to take Alexander, she shook her head, and then said to his mother, "Would like a cuddle?" She stood before Margaret had formed a polite refusal.

As she held Alexander out to James and Josie's mother with a proud smile, James felt every one of his muscles jam tight. His mother was not maternal. This was not going to end well.

His mother's face blanched. "I . . . I don't think so."

Marina smiled reassurance. "You raised two beautiful children, I'm sure you'll be fine with one more for a few minutes. He's really quite cuddly."

His father snorted with laughter. James turned to face him. His belly tightened and he felt . . . disturbed. He couldn't put his finger on why, but he was certain his dad's laughter had been meant to cut . . . to wound. To hurt.

"You're joking, right?" Edward asked Marina. "Margaret, with another child?"

James' mother surged to her feet. And this time her icy façade had splintered into a thousand deep cracks, her every raw emotion just about visible beneath.

Drawing a cloak of dignity around her and pulling it tight, his mother said tightly, "I'm afraid I've lost my appetite. You will all have to excuse me for a bit."

Marina retreated back to James, handing him Alexander who was wailing in her arms. She winced apologetically, and he placed a free hand over hers, giving it a squeeze. It was hardly her fault.

His mother's heels clacked away in one direction, as Marina walked with a soft tread in the other.

One escaped from a child, while the other hurried to feed and nurture.

"Well, that was awkward," his father mused. He pushed onto his feet. "Time for a drink."

James stood, gently rocking Alexander to settle him down. "You need to get some help for your addiction, Dad."

His father pivoted mid-step. "What did you say?"

"I said, you need help."

"How dare—?"

"I was a drug addict, Dad. I have a bit of an idea what you're going through. Trouble is, you don't just hurt yourself as an addict, you hurt those around you, too."

His dad blanched. "Drugs. You?"

"Yes."

"But . . . you've almost finished your training!"

He nodded, subduing a spurt of anger. His father worried more about the risk of losing his doctorate career, than his well-being and good health. "Yes. Don't worry. I'm off and have no intention going back."

Josie stood. "Dad, you're a practicing lawyer, and you're an alcoholic."

His father glared. "That's hardly the same!"

"Isn't it?" she asked, seemingly garnering strength of solidarity with James. "Do you really think anyone wants to be around you when you're drunk?" She didn't wait for an answer. Instead, flipping open her book, she began to read.

I'm not the 'me' you think I am
I'm not nice, no, and never when I drink
Ha! You wouldn't like me, I wouldn't think?
Peering deep into my wasted soul
And way beyond my everlasting smile
I'm not the 'me' you think I am
You don't know me, the real me . . . kept quiet
I give my secret loathing one more bite
While you chit and chat,
An endless rhythm, driveling this and that
I'm not the 'me' you think I am
Just one slit; the truth pulses from my vein
Releasing the toxin, my soul's inner stain
Then you'd see a whole world of hurt
My blood, your blood, discolored dirt
I'm not the 'me' you think I am
Be warned; don't venture inside my head,
The graphic images, wishing you were dead
My past, it becomes the hell of tomorrow
Happiness no longer something for borrow
I'm not the 'me' you think I am."
~Mel Teshco & Kylie Sheaffe

"You stupid girl," their father snarled. "A reformed mental patient." He turned to James. His lip curled. "And you, a drug addict!" He shook his head. "Of all the nerve, to have you two, lecturing me."

Marina returned, a fresh baby bottle in hand. She took Alexander from James and whispered, "I think I'd better take him somewhere quiet to feed. Will you and Josie be okay?"

James nodded. "We'll be fine." He smiled reassurance. Only when she withdrew did he stand and face down his father. "We're trying to help you, Dad. Trying to open your eyes."

His father's fists clenched, a muscle jerking to life in his jaw. "That's just it!" he roared. "I do not want my eyes opened. I want to be blind rotten drunk, blind to the things I don't want to remember, the things I've done!"

"What have you done, Daddy?" Josie asked, her voice young.

Their dad tipped his head back and closed his eyes, running shaky his hands over his face. "It wouldn't be a secret if I told, now would it?" He dropped his hands and expelled a noisy breath, directing a glare towards the direction his wife had made a hasty exit. "What is taking that woman, anyway?"

James flicked a look towards Josie. She nodded agreement to his silent question. He cleared his throat. "I think I'll go find her, see if she's alright."

His father had already turned his attention to the bar. "You do that."

James found his mother in her sewing room. She was leaning over the cutting table, her shoulders shaking, head in her hands. A book . . . an album, was pressed beneath her elbows.

"Mom, what's going on?"

She jerked her head up and swiped almost viciously at her eyes. "You shouldn't have come here," she said hoarsely.

"I'm your son. Why shouldn't I have come looking for you?"

"Oh, James," she whispered. She swiveled her chair around to face him, and he'd have sworn right then she was another person, another mother. The raw emotion he'd glimpsed earlier now churned behind her glistening eyes. A deep sadness lurked with grief and a bitterness she'd never been able to hide.

"Mom, tell me, please. Don't you see? These secrets have already all but torn our family apart."

She nodded. And it was as though the shutters were finally peeled back from her eyes, the floodgates opening as tears ran unchecked down her face. "Yes."

And along with her resignation came such great peace, James could almost touch it. Her tears were real.

She gestured for him to come close, then turned back in her chair to show him the album. Filling one page was a blown up black and white snapshot of Josie playing with her tea set, Maxwell sitting alongside an empty seat.

James released an unsteady breath. Even in black and white, there was no mistaking the retriever's link-chain dog collar.

"Josie loved to play make-believe, even back then," his mother said softly. "She'd sit for hours with her invisible friend, pouring tea from her toy tea set."

"Molly?" James asked. "To be honest, I'm not even sure anymore that Molly was a make-believe friend."

"I didn't say she had a make-believe friend, James. I said she had an invisible one."

He frowned, feeling a little out of his depth, unsettled and uncertain by his mother's odd behavior. "So . . . what are you saying?"

Some hair had come loose from her once perfect topknot, and her hand shook as she pushed some strands behind her ear. "I'm saying I had no choice but to deny the possibility all those years."

James felt giddy suddenly, like he was on the precipice of something profound, something life changing.

His mother flipped the album pages over to the very back. An old brown envelope dropped out. She carefully extracted the folded document within, and with a weary sigh, handed it to him.

"What's this?" He frowned, reluctant somehow to unfold and read the possible secrets to be found.

"James, please don't tell your sister," she implored. "It's . . . It's something I need to tell her myself."

He wanted to demand answers but somehow he couldn't force his gaze away from the document . . . couldn't scrape any words out of his throat. With single-minded intent, he focused downward.

His hands shook as he spread open the document, a tiny lock of blond hair pressed carefully within. "A birth certificate," he said hoarsely.

Chapter Seven

Josie watched her mother flick on the torch she'd carried with her from the car. The light blinded Josie for a moment, before it moved away to flash over James and then Marina, Alexander still sound asleep tucked up in Marina's arms.

Josie's pace slowed. She clutched the poetry book to her chest and all but waded through the thick, cold atmosphere of the cemetery. The night hours concentrated the vibrations in the air, heightened her awareness until she was almost overwhelmed with sensation.

A thick, crude wall appeared before them beneath the dull glow of a security lamp. Josie shivered a little. It was as if the wall had a life of its own, each block about to spill its own story.

Why would James bring her here, of all places? And for that matter, her mother? She hadn't avoided cemeteries all her life for nothing.

Her mother stopped by the wall. Josie's heart stilled, and then tripped over. Little wonder the blocks all but breathed. It was a cremation wall, filled with ashes of the dead.

The weak pool of light revealed her mother's drawn face, somehow capturing her dread, an echo of Josie's apprehension.

What was going on?

Josie hesitated beside her mother, and the torchlight dipped over the older woman as she pushed a hand into her tailored jacket pocket, the cherry-red color of her coat setting off a strange aura behind the beam.

"I asked James to bring us here, Jocelyn. I-I had to show you for myself."

Goose-bumps prickled Josie's skin. But for the moment at least it had little to do with this place for the dead. Even in her present state of mind, she recognized sheer strength of will in every set line of her mother's body.

She struggled for breath, gripped immediately by an acute rush of hypersensitivity. Whispers filled her mind. The light play of invisible fingers moved across her skin. Hollowness sucked at her belly, nausea creeping in fast.

She masked the reaction, though she knew whatever her mother was about to do was . . . big. "Show me what?" Margaret shifted the torchlight, past James and Marina, until the beam shone on her own outstretched hand, where inside a Ziploc bag a fine wisp of blond hair lay carefully preserved.

"Baby hair?" Josie whispered.

Margaret gave a jerky nod, careless of the tears slipping down her face. "Yes, just like the hair I saved from you when you were first born."

Josie's voice was barely audible as she placed her poetry book carefully on the ground and took hold of the bag. "Then . . . whose hair is this?"

James bent to read the etched writing aloud. "Molara Elizabeth Bowheart, 7th March, 1990."

Jocelyn shook her head. "But that's my birthday." She frowned. "Mother, you're scaring me."

Their mother's face crumpled. "I'm sorry, Josie. I couldn't live with the lie any longer. It hurts too damn much." She cleared her throat, though her voice barely came out above a whisper. "Molara was your stillborn twin."

Josie felt all the blood from her face drain. Her mouth dropped open, but nothing came out. Then a sudden, high-pitched scream pierced the thick silence, ending with the word, "Molly!" that echoed deep into the gloom.

"I'm so sorry, my darling. I'm so sorry," her mother said brokenly, her eyes awash with tears.

Josie barely heard as she subsided into hiccupping sobs.

She could only be grateful for James' strength as he pulled her into his arms in silent, grief-stricken commiseration.

She inhaled slowly, loudly, before she stepped back from James. Unclenching her hand, she carefully opened the bag. Cradling the fine strands close to her heart, she whispered, "Molly. My twin. My missing half."

She looked up abruptly, sensing immediately they weren't alone. She stared past her mother's shoulder as Molly appeared, her face sad, alone. "How did I—?" Josie shook her head, closing her eyes for a second to stop Molly thinking through her. "—I mean, how did Molly die?"

Her Mom began to shake, deep shudders that had undoubtedly been repressed far too long. "I'm so sorry . . . I didn't think I had a choice."

James put a hand on her shoulder. Small comfort right then. "What are you saying?" he demanded. "That our sister had a chance of life?"

"Yes."

It was a bullet straight to the heart only much, much more painful. Ice crept into Josie's veins, but she—and Molly—had to know, had to understand, no matter how painful for their mother. Josie stared at her mother, allowing fierce accusation to bubble up from the inside out. "Why?"

Her mother swallowed hard, noisily, her eyes and nose streaming. She managed a grateful nod when Marina moved forward for a moment to press a tissue into her hand. "You have to understand, I didn't have an easy pregnancy. I was sick all the time, couldn't keep food or even fluid down. Then when an ultrasound revealed one of my babies suffered from an abnormal heart, and was putting the other twin in jeopardy. I just . . . shut down. I was afraid, and it was all so overwhelmingly complicated."

James expelled a heavy breath, then explained it in layman's terms. "Acadiac MC twin. Molly would have been kept alive in the womb by Josie. Josie would have been pumping blood to Molly through the placental blood vessel connection."

"What does that all mean?" Josie whispered.

"It's called twin-twin syndrome, and with all the extra strain, Molly might well have unwittingly sent you into heart failure."

"So there was a chance Molly could have survived?" Josie asked starkly.

James declined to answer, instead giving their mother a chance to explain.

"My doctor encouraged me to eat well, stay hydrated and positive. She'd been monitoring us all closely. She offered me hope." Bitterness tinged her voice, "But Edward brought in a specialist doctor who didn't want to risk the life of both our girls. Right away I felt railroaded, pushed into doing something and quick."

"So you're saying Daddy agreed to terminate Molly?" Josie asked, her voice edging on furious.

"Molara," her mother corrected tiredly, "I chose the name, it means 'wished for child.' Your father refused to name her once his mind was made up. It was as if she never was, was never allowed to be."

Her mother shrugged, the gesture bone-deep weary. "Edward is a smart man, but he never once admitted Jocelyn and Molara could have been born alive and healthy, despite the specialists advice. I think he knew the legal and moral ramifications." She sighed. "A smart man, but so very, very torn."

Josie shook her head. "I can hardly believe it. And yet . . . it all makes so much sense." She looked up. "It's why Molly showed me the blood on his hands, isn't it? I'm not sure she understood it either, but now . . . now we both know the truth."

Her mother nodded mutely, seeming almost numb now to the pain.

A sudden breeze jostled around them, lifting Josie's hair. Alexander snuffled uneasily in his sleep.

Then Josie lifted her head and unclenched her hands. Margaret stepped forward, a whimper of denial forming as Molly's tiny, precious lock of hair lifted from her daughter's hand, hovered for a second, then swirled away, out of sight.

"What have you done?" her mother gasped.

Josie turned to her. "What you and Dad should have done years ago. I've set Molly free." She lifted her hands to the breeze and closed her eyes, rejoicing.

Then Josie's eyes flicked open. She and James shared a look before they turned simultaneously, focused intently in the same direction.

"Did you hear that?" James asked. Their mother shook her head even as Josie and Marina nodded. He let out a sigh. "A dog, it was barking."

"It's Maxwell," Josie breathed. "He's never far away from Molly. I think . . . I think he knows he's finally going home. He left me but in doing so he was always with Molly."

"Look!" James pointed at the pages of the poetry book that lay on the ground. They skipped open, shuffling one after the other, until the gust stilled, and the pages fell apart, laid open. Beckoning.

James moved forward, but Josie intercepted. "James, no."

Margaret put a hand to her mouth and Josie watched as Molly embraced their mother. Margaret would feel little more than something cool settling around her, but she'd have an idea she'd been forgiven. Molly had also just hugged her farewell.

Josie cleared her throat, her voice thick. "Molly wants me to read a poem. It's her way of saying goodbye." Their mother nodded, still a little disconcerted. "Of course."

Josie gave her a tentative smile. "Thank you." She retrieved the book, and under the weak pool of light she began to read.

The moon rises, the sun drops

Air breathes cold on your face.

Darkness; recurring dream never stops

Awake, I'm gone, and not a trace.

Don't cry. My spirit lives on.

My flame no longer dances
Memories will burn bright
No body, no voice, no second chances
And yet . . . I've seen the greater might
Don't cry. My spirit rejoices.
Confusion; belonging but not quite
Bound by invisible thread
And the light ahead so bright . . .
Calling to me, as homeward I'm led.
Don't Cry. My spirit is free.
My journey, one of pure love
No resentment, no concealing
Flowing freely from above
Forgiveness and love, my soul's healing
Don't cry. My spirit is home."
~Mel Teshco & Kylie Sheaffe

*

James left the car idling as he climbed out of the car at Marina's driveway and unbuckled Alexander from his baby capsule. He placed the sleeping baby in Marina's arms and murmured, "So much for dinner and an early night."

Marina shrugged a shoulder. "It doesn't matter. Your dad seemed relieved we called it off. Besides, I wasn't hungry anyway." She glanced at Alexander. "And my darling boy slept most of the night away."

James sighed. "I intend to make it up to you. Maybe I'll cook you an amazing barbeque dinner sometime soon?" At her relenting smile, he added, "You know, I really am sorry. About everything."

She placed a free hand on his shoulder. "It's not your fault. It's not anyone's fault."

"Yes, well, I think my dad has something to do with it."

She didn't say anything. She didn't need to. "Speaking of whom, you'd better get your Mom home. I'm sure she'll have some explaining to do about where we all disappeared."

He nodded. "Yes." He pressed a kiss to her soft mouth. "Would you like me to stay the night? When I get back home, that is."

Her smile glinted beneath the streetlight. "I'd like that. I'd like that a lot."

It was close to midnight by the time James pulled into the driveway of the Bowheart residence, and yet the big house was lit up like a Christmas tree.

Their mother turned to James and Josie as they climbed out of the car. "You really don't need to come in, I'll be fine."

Josie shut the passenger door with a decisive click. "We all know how Daddy can get with a few drinks. And now with this secret out . . ."

James stepped forward. "Josie is right. Besides, I have a bit of a favor I need to ask."

Their mother's laugh sounded forced. "Possibly not the best time to ask your father for any favors."

James shrugged, and then followed the women to the front door. "I know. But like it or not, I promised someone I'd speak to him on their behalf. It's not something that can wait."

Inside the fashionably overlarge living room, Josie announced, "Something really needs to be done about Daddy's drinking problem, if only he'd listen."

Margaret paused at the windows and looked out over the river. James wondered how much of the view she actually saw. She spun to face them, her slim shoulders stiff. "You think he'll never accept help, never give up drinking?"

Josie looked taken aback by her mother's question. Of course she would be shocked. Their mother never asked for anyone's opinion. Their dad appeared in the arched doorway then, giving Josie no time to answer. He swayed, his eyes bloodshot, his jacket off, shirt rumpled and tie askew. "Where did you lot get to? Last thing I knew we cancelled dinner, the next apparently my birthday is forgotten, too!"

Their mother stood firm, lifting her chin. "Our children wanted to say goodbye, Edward. As did I."

"What the bloody hell are you talking about, woman?" he growled.

James watched his parents' exchange. Just how long had they pretended a love neither felt? And what had caused their marriage to deteriorate so much? He inwardly shuddered. He guessed it didn't take a rocket scientist to realize it had all started from his sister's death.

He stepped forward. "Dad. We know everything."

His dad's usually closed expression revealed one emotion after the other. Surprise, discomfort, hurt, and finally . . . rage. Deep, toxic, soul-destroying rage. He turned on his wife. "Are you out of your mind?" he bellowed. "We agreed!"

Josie intervened, standing tall and unafraid. "No, Daddy. For the first time since Molly's death, she's totally sane."

Their father's lip curled. "So I suppose now I'm the big bad guy for seeing to it that one of my children lived?"

James felt hollow inside. He saw not one bit of remorse in his father's face, not one ounce of guilt in his voice. Just self-centered, stubborn pride. Anger suddenly filled him and rose inside, echoing his father's emotion. "You knew damn well there was a good chance both girls could have survived!"

"I didn't know that! None of us knew anything for sure, and we never, never will!" their father roared. And for the first time James saw something human glint beneath his father's stare. Guilt? Sorrow? Shame?

Their mother's heels clattered as she stalked towards her husband, sounding every bit like a feral animal turning on its hunter. "You. Didn't. Give. Me. A. Choice! You didn't care about us, only yourself. You never loved me! And God help me, every time I look at you all I see is the monster I call husband. A man poles apart to the one I married . . . the one I loved."

"You don't mean that." Their dad shook his head, clearly horrified. Rage had deflated from him, leaving him stark, helpless. "I-I'm not the monster you think I am."

Josie clasped her mother's arm, keeping her back, comforting her. She stared hard at her father. "Then tell us the truth, Daddy. Tell us what really had you so willing to sacrifice your own flesh and blood."

Their dad slumped against the wall, outspread hands covering his face, concealing his shame. And amidst the sudden silence, great, wracking sobs overtook his body, pushing him to the floor. "I did what I . . . what I thought I had to," he gasped. "I love you, Margaret, more than you know."

James could scarcely believe the thick emotions bruising the air. It was as though all their love, their anger, their doubts . . . all their years of emotion, was finally laid bare.

Their mother visibly swayed. "What about Molara?"

Their father grimaced, his face tortured . . . wounded. "One thing you despised right from the start about my family was the psychic ability passed along to each generation. Passed on to me." He turned to Josie as she let out a startled hiss. "Passed on to Josie."

Their dad finally swung a knowing look towards James. "And you, James."

James nodded. He wasn't about to deny it. Denial had led him nowhere but emotional withdrawal and the hell of drugs. A mirror of the man before him.

Their father released a heavy breath, then swiped a hand over his face. "I had a vision." He paused, seemingly gathering the courage to explain . . . to relive what he had seen. "Your mother's water broke, contractions following right after. Complications quickly arose." He sucked a breath between clenched teeth. "There was blood everywhere."

"Go on," their mother said, still and quiet, almost dignified, though her face was leached of color, her eyes round and stricken.

"I watched you, my wife, take your last breath as they tried to save you, but they couldn't stop the blood. Our twins were cut out from you in a last ditch attempt to save them . . . but they lay still, both dead. Their tiny bodies were taken away by the nurses. And you . . . you were left alone in all that blood, alone, declared dead."

Tears coursed down his cheeks. "I held you in my arms, Margaret, I cried my heart out for my wife, my girls. And the blood, it dripped through my fingers, reminded me of my loss."

"Oh . . . Daddy," Josie cried out. She raced over to him and threw herself into his arms. Wrapped together in shared emotion, shared love.

James' vision blurred as he turned away from the scene and focused on his mother. She turned to him, shock etched on her face as the reality of it all set in.

"He needs you," James found himself saying.

It was only when, some half an hour later as he pulled into his driveway with Josie half asleep beside him, that he realized he'd not gotten around to asking his dad about the favor for Tom.

Chapter Eight

Melbourne, Australia
    Dale-Smithson University,
    Sunday, July 31st
    "James Edward Bowheart."
    My turn.

James swallowed back a sudden attack of nerves, adjusted his black doctorate bonnet with its scarlet tassel, and stepped up onto the podium. At last, the day had arrived.

Everything seemed to slow, a still-life, frame-by-frame sequence shot as he looked out over the audience to focus on his family and friends.

Marina was beaming, Alexander tucked in her arms and sleeping again. Josie sat beside her, next to their parents. A few rows back, Tom sat with an arm around his fiancée, Stevie.

His father had really pulled a rabbit out of the hat for Tom. He'd gone with the heroic self-defense line, where Tom had saved the woman he loved. The jury had eaten it up, and soon after Tom had been acquitted.

A free man . . . a changed man. And though Tom had missed this opportunity to graduate, his time would come.

A few hours later, the graduation ceremony over and the group photos out the way, he headed over to his family.

Josie raced over, launching herself at him to hug him with a squeal of joy. "Well done, Doctor James!"

As she dropped to the ground, he shook his head and with a wry grin said, "Thanks, sis."

Marina was next, glowing with contentment. "I'm so proud of you."

James' face ached as he broke into yet another grin. This was one day he'd never forget, but it would be surpassed. "Still proud enough to be my wife in three weeks?" he asked, his grin now splitting his face.

She giggled, music to his ears. "Most definitely."

In three weeks time he would be a married man.

His very own, happily ever after.

His Mom and dad, their hands intertwined, moved towards him. It seemed since all the secrets about Molly had been exorcised, their love for each other had rekindled and grew day by day.

His mother's eyes shone. "A momentous day."

His father cleared his throat. "You've followed your heart, son. I commend you for it."

There was a new brightness behind his dad's eyes since he'd started attending AA meetings, an alertness and joy for life that shone right through.

James nodded. "Thanks."

He knew his parents were still not quite at the hugging stage, he only hoped time would see that change.

Robyn approached then. She looked so tiny, even with her swollen baby belly. She smiled, her face creasing with tender delight. "Congratulations James! My husband would have been—"

She gasped abruptly, her sentence cut short. She looked down, and James followed her stare. Fluid . . . and lots of it, puddled on the concrete between her high-heeled feet.

She looked up, her expression shocked, terrified. "James!"

He went straight into doctor mode, reassuring her even as he led her to his car in his full regalia kit of cloak and bonnet. She needed a hospital now, damn it!

"How many weeks along are you now?" he asked calmly, while inside his gut twisted in fear.

"I'm a few days over twenty-six weeks." Her face went bleached-bone white. "I want you there with me, James. Please. My husband had great faith in you and I-I trust in you, too."

"Of course."

How ironic to have so many doctors in one place, but none of the equipment necessary. Robyn would need to be taken to a neonatal intensive baby care unit and birthing suite. She'd need drugs to delay her birth, her baby's heartbeat monitored, and steroids to help her baby's lungs mature.

"Should we ring for an ambulance?" Marina asked.

He shook his head. "No. I'm not sure how much time she has."

He helped Robyn into the front seat of his car as Marina placed Alexander into his baby capsule at the back, before she clipped her own seatbelt on beside her son.

Checking Robyn was comfortable and calm, he made a mental note to buy a more family friendly car as he all but ran to the driver's side of his car.

His dad put a hand on his arm. "We'll follow you to the hospital, son. From there I can drive Marina and Alexander home."

James nodded. "Thanks, Dad. We'd appreciate that."

He had Marina ring the hospital to notify them as he pushed every speed limit on the road to get there on time and give Robyn and her baby every chance.

Robyn groaned, bending over double as an obvious contraction hit.

James pushed harder on the accelerator. "Run me through what you're feeling right now."

"The pain is bad, almost constant."

Shit!

"And before your water broke?" he asked.

Robyn gasped. Gritting her teeth, she admitted, "I woke up with a bad backache early this morning. I thought I'd slept wrong."

"No cramps, no blood spotting?"

"A few cramps the last few hours, but nothing terribly painful." She sucked in a short, sharp breath. "I had some blood spotting, but it was much earlier in my pregnancy."

And she'd told no one?

"The best thing you can do now for your baby is stay strong and calm. Focus on your breathing, stay positive, and—"

"It's coming!" She closed her eyes and fisted her hands until her knuckles were white. "James, I have to push!"

He braked, maneuvering the car to the side of the road and flicking on its hazard lights. This baby wasn't waiting for any hospital!

Like an epiphany, fragments of Robyn's words, read from her dead husband's journal, sounded in his head.

I saw a miracle today.

The tiny girl's spark of life couldn't possibly last.

The Mom refused to listen.

Instead, she channeled every ounce

Of her determination, every ounce of her love into her baby,

Her baby that she touched and held at every opportunity.

Her baby responded and fought for her little life . . .

She wasn't aware that it was impossible, she was surviving . . .

Goose-bumps erupted over his skin with the profound knowledge the professor was with him every step of the way, guiding him.

Marina moved to his side, ready to assist. His heart swelled as she helped him out of his bonnet and gown. I love her so much.

Then he was slipping into doctor mode, reclining the passenger seat backward, drawing off Robyn's underwear and tugging off her shoes to make her comfortable. He assessed her vital signs, and then nodded. "Your baby is impatient to see the world."

Robyn's eyes filled with moisture, pain etched into her expression. "But I'm too early," she said through gritted teeth, a strained tone that could mean only one thing.

James nodded. "Your time is now. You have to be strong. You have to keep the faith."

Robyn gasped in a breath. Her eyes turned inward, unfocused. "Oh, James. My darling husband, I will . . . I am."

Marina shot him a startled look, but didn't make comment on Robyn's talking to her dead husband. Instead she concentrated on the task at hand. "I've got some cloth nappies in Alexander's bag."

"Perfect," he agreed.

She'd have made a great nurse, he thought. Then Robyn gasped, clearly distressed as another labor pain rushed her back to lucid awareness.

He had a job to do.

Moments later, crying out long and loud, Robyn pushed hard.

In a sudden wave of motion, the baby slipped out, and James was holding the slick, tiny body of Robyn's son in his hands. "It's a boy," he announced past the lump in his throat.

Robyn's whole body shook with suppressed joy and shock. "Is . . . is he okay?"

James experienced one millisecond of amazed wonder, before reality returned like a giant wave dumping him under.

The baby didn't cry. He was fragile, tiny, and weak. And James noticed immediately his breathing was erratic and unstable. He had Robyn undo the buttons on her blouse, and then with the umbilical cord still attached, he rested the baby on Robyn's chest.

Skin on skin. Heartbeat to heartbeat.

Marina wrapped a cloth nappy over the baby's tiny, bloodied form. Even folded, the infant was almost lost underneath.

"Hold him tight," James instructed Robyn. "We've got to get you both to the hospital."

Without the necessary drugs to administer, he worried about the baby's underdeveloped organs, particularly his lungs. Cutting the umbilical cord could wait, and in fact, the infant may well benefit from the extra stem cells and cord blood that even now pulsed from mother to baby.

The passenger door clicking shut, he gave Marina a quick squeeze and whispered, "I love you," before they clambered into their seats.

Merging back into the traffic, he was belatedly aware his parents and Josie had pulled in behind them. They'd hung back from the crisis, clearly realizing they'd only have gotten in the way.

A pediatrician, neonatal nurse, and midwife waited for them when they arrived. In a flurry of activity they put Robyn, together with her infant son, onto a stretcher and wheeled them on ahead.

Marina smiled reassurance. "Go, James, we'll be fine. Robyn needs you."

He gave her a brief, hard kiss, before he let her go. "Thank you." *My angel.*

Then he was following the hive of activity through the front doors and into the birthing suite.

Some of the nurses were gowning up, worry creasing their faces. Pulling on sterile gloves, he nodded to them. A few of them would know Robyn, or at the very least would have seen her with the professor before his death.

One of the nurses already in the birthing suite opened the door and gestured to him. "Robyn is asking for you."

He followed her through the doors and immediately saw Doc Moore leaning over Robyn, a pair of umbilical clamps in hand. A nurse waited close by with a pair of scissors.

Robyn shook her head. "No. No!" She turned frantic eyes to James. "I want James! James is my doctor."

Doctor Moore turned his hard stare on James. "He has no authority here."

James took a step forward, his jaw working hard at this man's stupid ignorance. "Are you refusing the rights of this patient?"

Doc Moore's expression tightened. "Your role right here, right now, is as a support person for the patient. Nothing more. Do we have that clear?"

James nodded, smothering a glare. "Of course."

*

Robyn tried to will calm. But as the older doctor turned her baby onto his back and then clamped and cut the cord, panic crashed inside her chest like a blackbird seeking escape. This cutting of the cord was a final separation, the snip of tender flesh an irreversible severance from her child.

My darling husband, how I wish you were still here.

He would have made certain of their baby's future. He would have held their son in his arms. Safe. Invincible. He would have been their rock, like always.

She focused on her baby's tiny chest, searching for a rise and fall. Her heart squeezed tight, horror almost suffocating her voice. "He's not breathing! Is he breathing?"

Almost immediately, and without ceremony, one of the team plucked him from her grasp. James' hand covered hers, and she clung to him like a lifeline, watching as they took her tiny baby away from her and placed him into a trolley.

James squeezed her hand "It's okay. They're giving him oxygen to help him breathe."

"Is he going to be okay?" Panic edged into her voice. "Tell me he is going to be alright!"

She saw him frown a little, as if unsure how to answer. Then the midwife said, "Just a little sting."

Robyn jerked as the needle pricked her thigh, aiding the release of her placenta. But she cared little about the pain, little about herself at all. It was all about her baby.

Snippets of conversation were all too loud and clear. "Deflated lungs. A hundred percent oxygen. Possible brain bleed."

And in a flurry of movement, her baby was wheeled out of the room . . . out of sight.

"James, is that as bad as it sounds? What's happening?"

"They've taken him to the neonatal ICU to be monitored. They're doing everything they can."

She started to shake, and knew shock had well and truly kicked in. "James, go with them. Please? You must."

The midwife frowned, the lines in her brow deepening as James nodded. "Of course. I'll see what I can find out."

It was only minutes, or perhaps hours, later that James came back. His brave face didn't fool her one bit. "What is it? Tell me!"

The other doctor followed. And even in her state of panic and shock, she sensed the silent animosity swell between them. "Mrs. Newton," he greeted formally. "I'm afraid the news isn't great."

She suppressed a pained gasp. She wouldn't fold and break now. She couldn't. She was a Mom now, with a baby who needed her. "News?" she managed.

"Your baby's lungs collapsed and had to be inflated. Right now he's on a hundred percent oxygen. To be honest, it could go either way, but you should prepare yourself for the fact he may not make it through the night."

She swallowed back denial. "I want to go and see him."

The doctor nodded. "Of course."

When the doctor left, James went and found her a wheelchair. He rolled her into the NICU beside her baby's humidicrib.

She pressed her lips together, stifling a sob. "He's so tiny," she said hoarsely.

She leaned over, putting a hand into the open humidicrib, where warmth from the heating light above radiated downward. She brushed her forefinger along the soft red skin of her son's arm. "Hello, James Edward Junior."

Little James Junior chose that moment to open his eyes, staring directly at her.

"I love you, little man," she whispered.

James crouched beside her, focused intently on the readings. He blew out an awed breath and pointed to the oxygen saturation meter. "Look at that."

Robyn stared at the meter, watching the reading spike from ninety-one to ninety-five percent.

"That's remarkable," said James. "His saturations are improving."

"He's watching me," Robyn breathed, beyond amazed now. Her heart swelled, love for this tiny baby almost overwhelming yet growing minute by minute. "He knows I'm here. He's connecting to my touch."

"I do believe you're right," James said, a smile in his voice. "He's a little fighter."

Robyn nodded, a shiver moving up and down her spine. "He's going to be a great man one day, just like his father." She turned and looked up at him. "And like his godfather, if you'll accept."

James eyes went wide. He nodded, a grin breaking out. "I'd be honored, incredibly honored."

She smiled. "Thank you, James. I know my husband would have approved."

James straightened, and she knew he was moved as he fought back tears. "That means the world to me." His gaze stole back to the humidicrib. "Hang in there, little James, I have to go. But I'll be seeing you again very soon."

James paused at the doors, his attention all on the baby. "And just so you know, little guy, no James Edward I know ever gives up."

It was late by the time James rang for a taxi and had the driver drop him home.

The lights were out at Marina's. It'd been a big day for her and Alexander, and he wasn't about to disturb her now, however much the thought of going over there and taking her into his arms sounded like his own piece of heaven.

He kept the lights off at his house when he slipped inside, collapsing onto his favorite recliner. He closed his eyes and was instantly transported to another time, another place that had lay too long dormant in his memory.

The single flame from a crude torch cast light on the blood-soaked dirt floor. A thin, once colorful blanket beneath the new mother's dark, stick-thin legs, was thick with the crimson gush of new life.

Doctor Lowe abstractedly swiped at a whining cloud of mosquitoes as he nodded at James. "We'll clamp and cut the cord later."

James helped the doctor pass the infant girl to the weary mother. The baby was tiny and malnourished, but she instantly responded to her mother's loving touch, who cradled her baby against her.

James let out a breath, rubbing his bloodied hands across the back of his khaki pants. "I didn't think the baby had any hope."

The doctor nodded. "You'll get used to seeing the miracle of birth around here. In our culture, a baby this small, in these conditions, would not be expected to live. I often wonder about the wisdom of modern medicine, separating a mother from her ill baby at birth when the baby needs her most."

As James came back to the present, it was the professor's words that echoed in his head.

I've actually made similar observations as well as many other unscientific happenings over the years.

James jerked onto his feet and flicked on the light. Weariness slid off him like an old blanket as he retrieved the professor's journal and flipped open its first page.

Every word, every sentence, every paragraph was gold. The professor's experiences, his learning's and his beliefs, a lifetime of his work in James' hands.

Dawn light was cracking through the curtains when a tread on the floorboards had him jerk his head up. "Josie. What are you doing awake?"

Her long hair mussed, her eyes still drooping with sleep, she carried her poetry book like it was all that mattered as she peered at him and said, "I did get some sleep, unlike you."

He closed the journal carefully, and then stretched his arms out to his sides, arching his spine. "I got a little absorbed in the professor's written observations."

But Josie was taking little notice. She stared past him, looking puzzled. "I just saw the oddest thing."

"Oh?"

"A kangaroo and her joey, hopping around our living room."

"Ah." James didn't even question her visions anymore. "Strangely enough, the professor made detailed notes about a special kind of infant preemie care, now known as kangaroo care. He was a big advocate of human touch."

Josie pulled herself together. "It makes sense. And we know firsthand what it was like to be brought up without hugs, without any displays of affection and love."

"I can't help but think about how Robyn's baby responded right after he was born. I laid him on her chest, skin on skin, umbilical cord still attached. The moment we got to hospital and they separated them, he went downhill fast."

"Oh, James. I hope he's going to be okay."

He looked at her hard. "Do you think there was a deeper reason behind your vision, a connection somehow?"

"I think so, yes." She frowned, thoughtful. But he knew she wasn't thinking, she was . . . seeing. "Her doctor, he's not a good man. His energy isn't helping."

"I know."

She opened her poetry book. "That doctor . . . this is what I see."

Look at you—what do I see?

Exterior, brave face, with smile stretched wide.

But you're fading inside; unwell. You can't fool me.

Hiding your true self, blocking your own tide . . .
Look within. Face yourself, your demons. Don't give in.
A lovely face, dimples; white, perfect teeth,
Buff body, working out till you're awash with sweat.
What's this—a distraction from all that hides beneath?
Your worldly goals, your desires, all have been met.
Look within. Is this what you want? Never surrender.
Big white mansion by the sea, piles of money to burn,
Stocks and bonds, shares and investments, a finger in every pie.
The envy of many, it's what you crave. But love . . . you spurn.
Inside you're miserable, unhappy, all compassion has died.
Look within. What happened to your dreams? Stop! Think again."
~Mel Teshco

James pushed onto his feet. "I've got to go to Robyn and her son, don't I?"

Josie nodded. "I think so, yes."

*

Robyn lay under the scratchy blanket of the hospital bed, wholly content at the soft warmth of her tiny baby snuggled under her nightgown, against her chest.

Her breasts tingled, her milk stimulated by this close contact. This kangaroo care her husband had once spoken about in such glowing terms.

He was right.

The distant cry of a baby sounded. Her baby. She froze, disbelieving. Then her hands were brushing up and down her torso. There was nothing but air, her nightgown pushing flat against her barren, stone-cold belly.

Terror stole her voice. "Where's my baby?"

Then the cry again, much closer now, if only she could see. Frantic, she peered into the impenetrable darkness with its swirling, eerie mist.

Why hadn't I noticed this before?

The cry sharpened, louder and so very close. And like a flick of a switch, a beam of light from the heavens above shone down. So close yet so far away.

She could see her baby now, swathed in brilliant luminosity, and rising slowly upward, towards the ever-brightening light.

She stretched out an arm. No! Please, God. No!

An overriding sense of urgency filled her. She couldn't bring her baby back physically. Only her will alone, her love would save him.

Her heart suddenly burned hot in her chest. She gasped, looking down, away from her baby for just one second. Her heart glowed through her skin; she could see its every beat in her chest, rippling outward.

She turned back to her baby, whose little body was moving ever upward. "James," she whispered. "It's not your time to go."

All-consuming love lit her up completely, saturating her every cell before concentrating right into the core of her heart. Her spine abruptly arched. A path of light shot directly from between her chest to her baby, coiling around him and drawing him gently downward.

She reached up, straining to reach him, her whole mind, body and soul focused on bringing him back when suddenly the connection was severed.

A nurse gently shook her awake.

Robyn blew out a relieved breath. Thank goodness, it was just a dream.

"The doctor is with your baby. He wants to talk to you."

Wakefulness slammed into her like a body blow. "He does?" She swung her legs to the side of the bed, shaking her head to the wheelchair the nurse had with her. "No. No, I'm fine. I can walk."

The nurse nodded. "If you're sure."

The doctor looked up at her approach, his expression betraying nothing more than a man with a lot of patients to see in too short a time.

"You wanted to see me?" she asked.

"Yes." He set aside the clipboard in his hands. "I'm afraid your son has taken a bad turn."

Her legs were suddenly unsteady, and she understood the nurse's offer of a wheelchair. "How bad?"

"We nearly lost him a few times."

The vivid, powerful dream she'd had seemed suddenly all too real. She focused on her baby, lying motionless and so frail in his humidicrib. "He . . . he's okay now, though?"

"Ah. Well, statistically we're looking at a child who may never walk, who may suffer with blindness or even cerebral palsy. Mrs. Newton, Your child may well have severe brain damage. The situation is very precarious."

James walked through the doors like a breath of fresh air, and somehow his presence steeled her spine, hardened her resolve.

James had clearly overheard at least part of the doctor's spiel. He shook his head. "That's all they are. Statistics."

The doctor glowered. "Unfortunately, statistics don't lie!"

"Where there's hope, there's life," Robyn whispered, appalled by this doctor's lack of compassion, lack of optimism, and faith.

The doctor sighed, clearly acknowledging a mother's love for her child, but just as clearly unwilling to partake in the emotional roller coaster ride. "I suggest you think seriously about his funeral arrangements. Perhaps you'd like an hour with him?"

"Yes. I . . . I want to hold him."

The doctor relented with a stiff nod. "And then we'll need to make some decisions."

Decisions?

Her voice sounded strangled. "Are you implying that my decisions, based on your statistics, might lead to my son having his life support switched off? Are you asking me to consider turning off his oxygen?"

Somehow she couldn't cry. It was as though all her inner strength fought against the hopelessness of her son's future.

The doctor frowned disapproval. "We may not have a choice. His brainwaves indicate very little activity."

James stepped forward. "There is always a choice. And I'd like to suggest you run some more EEG tests right after Robyn has her time with her son."

The other doctor's jaw tightened. "I see no need to run tests yet again."

James measured his words, looking and sounding every inch in control. "The late professor documented the advantages of kangaroo care. The sickest of infants in the most primitive situations thrived from a mother's touch."

The doctor curled a lip. "So the professor's progeny is now telling me how to run my ward?"

"Not at all. I just didn't want to waste thirty years of intensive research, with findings showing infants using this kangaroo care can have a reduction in oxygen requirements, increased oxytocin levels, no apneas or bradys, more stable heart rate, and more spontaneous respiration—"

The doctor swiped out a hand. "I've heard enough."

James didn't back down. "I just want you to allow the possibility. You have nothing to lose and everything to gain. The ball should be in Robyn's court."

Robyn let out a heavy breath. "Just let me hold my baby. Please."

The doctor nodded, resigned. "Very well."

It took some minutes for the staff to roll in a gurney bed, positioning it right alongside James Junior.

Robyn adjusted the headrest and made herself comfortable, before James carefully lifted the infant out of the humidicrib and passed him to her, the nurse taking care of the monitor and tubes still attached.

Her little James moved on his own then, one fragile arm stretching out, and his five tiny fingers resting on one of her breasts.

Everyone around her faded out, her eyes—her whole being—on her baby. He was so tiny and frail, but he was a fighter through and through. She only wished the doctor understood that, too.

"Mommy's got you now," she whispered. "Mommy's got you."

Her little boy's eyes opened, connecting with her. She swallowed, her heart melting. It was as though he knew this shared moment was monumental, special.

Do or die.

"Hi there, little guy," she crooned. "Mommy loves you so much." An all-consuming force inside willed her infant to fight, to live.

She gently ran a thumb pad along his back, carefully avoiding all the tubes. His skin was so delicate and soft to the touch. "You really are a fighter, aren't you?"

James motioned towards the ventilator meter, advising the doctor, "He's already breathing easier."

The doctor frowned, then said, "I'm late for rounds." He gave Robyn a nod. "Perhaps we'll see how your son goes through the night."

Pure joy bubbled within, evaporating all other emotion and pushing the cold right out of the room. "Thank you."

The battle had been won, but the war had just started.

Her hand was squeezed. She looked down, but no one could have possibly touched her. No one tangible, at least. She smiled. Her husband would be proud.

She looked at James. "Thank you."

He grinned, utterly relieved. "Anything for my godson." The machine bleeped as he sat beside Robyn. He leaned towards James

Junior and announced, "Besides, I have your father's journal waiting for you."

Sudden warmth surrounded Robyn, peace settling over her like a much loved and well-worn coat. A powerful certainty followed soon after.

She turned to James, just as he twisted to face her, a look of wonder on his face.

He feels it, too.

Exchanging knowing grins, she said with utter conviction, "He's going to make it."

Chapter Nine

Toorak, Australia

Sunday, August 20th

James Edward Bowheart plucked at his ruby tie for what seemed the hundredth time in perhaps ten minutes, wishing he could tear it off.

Breathe.

Who'd have thought me, uncomfortable in a suit?

He took a slow, steadying breath, putting a lid on his nerves and distracting himself by inspecting the church in a slow perusal.

The beautiful stained windows, depicting the exact same scene he remembered as a child, glowed faintly beneath the mid-afternoon sky. Dust motes floated regally in the single ray of light coming through the glass, the scent of wax and roses strong in the air.

The church was packed with guests. He peered harder. There were a few he didn't recognize. At the front, Robyn sat alone and dignified, her slim shoulders pushed back in her floral print dress, a string of pearls around her throat.

She'd been so strong, so courageous. Little wonder the professor had loved her without restraint.

His parents sat beside Robyn. Edward held Margaret's hand. They were both clearly in love and happy, perhaps for the first time since their marriage.

Marina's aunt sat in the opposite pew, deftly jiggling a restless Alexander. He nodded at her, grateful she'd stepped up to the babysitting plate.

Murmurs suddenly filled the church.

Marina was here.

He swallowed another attack of nerves, turning to his sister who waited at the side stage. She raised her violin towards her chin, tossing him a smile of reassurance. Then her bow moved over the strings and the beautiful, exquisite notes of "You Raise Me Up" filled the church.

Marina glided down the aisle towards him, radiant in her silk off the shoulder dress, walking alone. Strong. Poised.

Her father had declined the invitation to give her away, and Marina had decided no bridesmaids. No flower girls.

Just him and her, starting their journey together.

She stood before him, her eyes glistening behind her veil.

"I love you," he mouthed.

Then the reverend stepped forward, and James and Marina repeated their vows. The reverend looked up at the couple before him, citing a bible verse they'd carefully chosen.

"Love is patient, love is kind, it does not envy, it is never boastful, nor conceited, nor rude, never selfish, not quick to take offense. There is nothing love cannot face, there is no limit to its faith, its hope, and endurance. In a word, there are three things that last forever: faith, hope, and love, but the greatest of them all is love."

At the reverend's nod, James gently lifted Marina's veil and kissed her beautiful mouth, all the while knowing that with every atom of his being, his life was now perfect.

He walked her back down the church aisle in something of a joyous haze, only vaguely aware of the beautiful, happy piece played by Josie.

Outside, not a cloud marred the bright azure sky. The guests swarmed through the double doors in their wake, pitching great handfuls of garish confetti into the air so that it rained down on them, clinging to their hair, their clothes.

Marina abruptly giggled, skipping down the steps in her high heels like a newborn filly on wobbly legs.

Robyn intercepted them before the photographer could claim their attention. Though her face was bruised with weariness, she radiated joy at their special occasion.

"I'm so proud of you both. You were made for each other." She kissed them each on the cheek before pulling back, her expression growing serious. "I wish I could stay for the reception, but my James needs me."

Marina's dimples showed as she smiled, her hands coming to rest on Robyn's slender shoulders. "We totally understand. Just be sure to say hello to that gorgeous boy for me!"

James slipped an arm around Marina. "Thanks for coming, Robyn. It means a lot to us."

Then they were all but carried along in the tide of well wishers, and he lost sight of her through the crowd.

They posed for photos—a tired and grumpy Alexander featuring in many of them—when James saw Josie escape the last of the family wedding portraits.

All her attention appeared snared by a woman standing back from the throng.

Josie nodded another absent-minded thank you at yet another face in the crowd who complimented her musical talent. But there was only one face she was drawn to, one she'd recognized right away, despite the years that had passed.

The older woman, still so lovely and elegant, watched her approach. She stepped forward, meeting her partway. "Hello, Jocelyn."

Josie released a little breath, her stomach fluttering with strange nerves when she enquired faintly, "Connie Anderson?"

The other woman nodded. "I did wonder if you'd recognize me after all this time."

Sudden self-doubt settled inside Josie. Clearly her vision all those years ago, at this very church, had been wrong! Connie was walking proof she'd been mistaken.

An apology formed on her lips, just as the older woman's face softened, exuding warmth. Connie opened her arms and enfolded Josie into a hug. Pulling back, Connie looked her up and down, murmuring, "You're so beautiful, so . . . whole. Certainly not the broken girl I remembered so well."

Josie flushed a little at Connie's intensity, her kindness. "It's been a long journey, but I did get there in the end."

"So I see."

Josie glanced around. "Is Mr. Anderson here? It's been a while, I probably wouldn't recognize him anymore."

Connie exhaled sharply, and Josie's attention rocketed back to her. Goose-bumps erupted over her skin even before seeing the other woman's pale face. "Are you okay?"

"You mean, your mother didn't tell you?"

Josie frowned, until the pieces fell together. She wrapped an arm around the older woman and led her back inside, though she was unsure who supported whom. In unison, they sank onto the pew.

Josie held Connie's glistening stare. "Your husband died, didn't he?"

Connie's next words crashed around her just as hard as the rock fall in her vision so long ago. "Yes . . . at El Capitan."

A tear trickled down Connie's powdered cheek. Her smile was little more than a grimace as she shrugged, her intricate lace shawl pulling tight across her slender shoulders. "He thought you were seeking attention, heaven only knew you got so little."

Josie nodded, distantly wishing there was more she could have done, but comforted by the fact she'd done the best she knew how at the time.

"There you are!"

Josie twisted on the hard wooden pew, just in time to see her mother clatter to a stop, a dawning look of utter horror replacing her joyous expression.

Josie sighed. Holding a grudge wasn't part of her makeup. Life was just too short, a blip on the universe radar.

And sometimes one had to focus on the good stuff if they ever wanted to find true happiness. "It's okay, Mom. Connie told me what happened."

Margaret nodded, lips pulled taut. "I couldn't tell you," she whispered. "I didn't want you to know. I didn't want to accept the possibility myself, let alone encourage even more visions."

Connie stood. "Your daughter has a gift, Margaret. You should be proud of her. If she hadn't stood up and told me what she saw, despite the punishment you no doubt measured out, I'd be dead now, right alongside my husband."

Josie leaned back on the hard pew, feeling faint. "I'm not bad," she whispered.

Margaret nodded. "I'm so sorry, Jocelyn." She turned at the heavier tread of her husband behind her. She held a hand out towards him.

When he accepted and moved close, Edward acknowledged hoarsely, "We both are, Jocelyn, we both are."

James took his seat beside Marina on the huge balcony overlooking the Yarra River. He couldn't help but wonder if his parents' house had ever looked so good, ever looked so homey.

Twilight had begun to settle around them, and the hundreds of fairy lights had been switched on, sparkling around the pillars, the trellises at either end, the private jetty at the wide river below.

A cool breeze ruffled the treetops, billowing Marina's long red-gold hair. He thumbed a strand back behind her ear, giving into the adoration that filled him from the inside out. "Did I tell you how much I love you?" he murmured.

She smiled, her attention his alone. "I don't mind hearing it again."

Someone nearby cleared their throat. They pulled apart, their hands intertwined. The speeches were about to begin.

Tom stood, and soon had everyone in stitches with his childhood anecdotes he'd shared with James. Marina's aunt stood next, contributing enough glowing praise for the newlyweds to almost squirm with self-consciousness.

Most unexpected though, was seeing Josie come to her feet. She glanced at Matt, who gave her an encouraging smile.

James decided his sister looked like a princess in her sleeveless, coffee-colored dress, its bodice hand stitched with flowers, her hair spilling past her shoulders like a silver waterfall.

Margaret clacked a spoon against one of her precious crystal glasses, shushing any chatter. "My daughter has something to say," she announced.

Josie smiled, and then spread her poetry book open on the table to the page she'd book-marked. "Some months ago a lonely, terrified girl was given a gift on her birthday by her brother. That gift became the light in my darkness."

The guests were silent, all eyes trained on the woman most would remember as a sensitive young girl with unsaid mental issues.

"That brother was James, and that girl, of course, was me. I came to understand the deeper meaning of the written word, began to embrace the power of believing."

She caught James' stare. "It became routine to read a poem from the book, a poem that developed into so much more than mere words alone." She glanced around the room. "Tonight, I'd like to share one of these poems."

If love said, 'Listen to me,' what would it have to say?
Hear not the word that causes pain
For I do not speak in such a way
But I am right in front of you, within you and around
I know you say you want me, but yet you haven't found
That I'm in the tender kisses your child gives you every day,
If you'd just stop and feel the warmth of my subtlest displays
You should not seek to understand me, for that can never be
But instead I wait here patiently until again you see
That either love is real and fear is not, or the visa versa
One day I hope you choose my truth and no longer have to suffer
For then you'll need to look no more, your fears will melt away
For they are but illusions that were born upon the day

The day you had no time for me or what I had to say.
So see, I have no hidden agenda and what I say is true
My secret yet so simple, a treasure trove for you
To receive beyond your wildest dreams, there's one thing you must conceive
Listen for my whisper, in true love you must believe!"
~Kylie Sheaffe

As Josie sat to a stirring round of applause, Matt giving her hand a squeeze, hired waiters moved through the open glass doors, bringing out the first-course entrée.

Edward stood. "Thank you, Jocelyn. That was a beautiful piece." He winked, and Josie exchanged a wry grin with James. They both understood their father was thinking back on the poem Josie had read to him about four months ago, highlighting his drinking problem.

Edward raised his glass of mineral water. "And now, I'd like to propose a toast to James and Marina."

James caught Marina close as the guests repeated Edward's toast.

Edward turned to his daughter. "And to my precious daughter's continued good health and happiness." He snared Margaret's gaze. "And my wife's continued support and love."

The guests erupted into more applause. James swallowed past the lump in his throat. He raised his own glass of mineral water. "Thank you, Dad."

An hour later, as the sounds of a bridal waltz drifted from the outdoor speakers, James drew Marina into his arms and onto the balcony floor reserved for dance space. Edward and Margaret moved out onto the floor then, followed soon after by Josie and her good friend, Matt.

Marina looked up at James. "It looks like Matt has resolved much of his past, too, if the easy closeness he shares with your sister is anything to go by."

James glanced over at them, seeing all too clearly Matt's relaxed expression, his almost carefree posture as he led Josie around the floor. "I think you're right, darling. I think he's learned to accept himself for who he is, just like we all have."

The song ended. When the next song started, almost all the wedding guests came out onto the floor. It was only a few hours later, when the evening was winding down, that James and Marina made their way to Edward and Margaret, who were silently dancing, cheek-to-cheek.

It was almost seemed a shame to interrupt them. He had never seen this level of intimacy from them before. Not once.

James put a hand on his dad's shoulder. "Mom. Dad. We're just about ready to call it a night."

Edward grinned. "The honeymoon is calling, eh, son?"

James felt somehow boyish, a flush climbing his neck, warming his cheeks. "We'd like to bring out Josie's surprise."

Margaret drew back. "Are you sure this is the right thing to do? She might not be ready—"

Edward shook his head. "Oh, she's ready. More than ready. It's past time now we all moved on, hmm?"

James watched his Mom take a deep, steadying breath, taking the leap of faith right alongside her husband. "Of course, dear. You're right." She turned to James and Marina. "You are all right."

Edward gave his wife a brief, hard kiss on the lips, and then spun on his heel to retrieve Josie's surprise. Only when he saw his father return a few minutes later, did he indicate for the music stop.

Into the silence James announced, "Thank you everyone for coming tonight, and for celebrating our special day. Marina and I are almost ready to call it a night and leave for our honeymoon."

To cheers and whistles, he exchanged a grin with Marina and added, "But first, I would like to present something to my sister."

Josie stepped forward. "James, it's your wedding, I don't expect anything!"

She stopped talking as Edward came forward, carrying a lidded cane basket. He put it on the table and stepped back. "Don't you want to take a look?" he encouraged.

Josie swallowed anxiety and managed a nod. All these months she'd learned to take control of her life, learned how to flick an off/on switch to her visions, her abilities. Now she wished she'd been more prepared. Gut instinct told her this was big, life-changing.

She swallowed, forcing her unsteady hands to unlatch the lid. She peered down. Something glinted inside. Maxwell's collar? Then a golden-furred head surged towards her, a little yap of excitement preceding the little pink tongue that slurped wetly across her chin.

"A puppy!" she squealed.

Edward beamed. "A golden retriever. He's all yours. All you have to do is name him."

Self-doubts and fears melted away like yesterday's news. She scooped up the wiggling puppy into her arms, cuddling him tight.

"Aren't you gorgeous!" she crooned. Tears prickled her vision as she looked up at her family, all of them with wide smiles splitting their faces. "I never dreamed I'd have another dog. Thank you."

The puppy squirmed some more, legs kicking as he tried so hard to lick her face. She laughed at his antics. "Look at you, silly thing! But you're so noble, too." She stared into his intelligent face. "Noble. What a perfect name."

And oddly, one that tugged at her senses.

James gave her a quick hug. "Great choice."

Marina kissed her. Patting Noble on his silky head, she murmured doggy speak to him about how much he'd get along with Rocco.

James chuckled. "I don't think you'll miss us too much while we're away, not with Noble occupying your time."

Josie kept hold of her puppy as James and Marina said their goodbyes. But it was only as they walked out of her field of vision that her internal switch flicked on, almost of its own volition.

Radiating out in front of her, like a real-life movie, she saw James as a much older man. He walked up onto a stage, accepting a medal for his achievements.

She leaned forward, peering at the medal. Then her vision panned in and she clearly saw engraved into the gold, a woman with a book on her lap, collecting water from a nearby rock. And an inscription she didn't understand.

Inventas vitam juvat excoluisse per artes.

And yet, she knew exactly what the medal represented. A shiver chased goose-bumps over her body as she whispered in awe, "The Nobel prize."

Chapter Ten

James stared hard at Marina, clutching her veined hands in his as a well of tears threatened to break past his rheumy eyes.

Age hadn't distilled his love for her. Indeed, it had strengthened it infinitely. Marina, his family, had been the source of his strength, the fuel to keep going these last few months.

His whole body shook with effort as he turned his head to peer at the nightstand. The Nobel Prize medal for medicine sat in pride of place, alongside the professor's ageing journal.

James Junior had brought him the leather book with the idea he'd be able to read it while he was bed-bound. A lovely gesture, which meant a great deal to him, but mattered little.

He'd memorized the professor's journal word-for-word. There was nothing in there he needed to read, its only value being the nostalgia of seeing the professor's handwriting.

He forced his head back, squinting at his aged wife, so beautiful even now, a few years past eighty. "My love, I'm not long of this earth now."

She shook her head. "Don't say that, James. Please. I can't let you go. We belong together."

"I'll be waiting for you in heaven, my love. You can be sure of that."

He forced his lungs to expand, to take in oxygen. Talking was an effort and had left him weak. He was only glad he'd be able to die at home, peacefully, surrounded by his beloved family.

Josie stepped forward, opposite Marina, and clutched his other hand.

James managed a smile for his little sis. She'd married a wonderful man who loved her unconditionally, and who'd encouraged her passion for music, for helping others. She'd used all her inheritance to fund a music school for both disadvantaged and gifted pupils. With the help of Marina, it was now one of the world's premier music schools.

"James." Josie's voice wobbled with emotion. "Thank you for everything. If it wasn't for you—"

"No. Thank you, Josie. You opened my eyes."

His stare moved over everyone in the room. Marina, Josie, Alexander, the younger James, who looked so much like the professor now.

Another young woman stood beside his bed, and though she was unfamiliar, her big eyes were filled with sorrow even as her inner warmth reached out and touched him, gave him comfort. She was precious to him, each of the people in the room were. "You all did."

Marina blinked back tears. "You've made us proud, James. You've done everything you've dreamed of and more than the professor could ever have asked and hoped."

James felt his heart expand, a burst of new life reviving him for just a few moments longer. "Thank you, my love. I did my best."

Josie squeezed his hand, and turned to look at his medal. "You've lived by your Nobel's code." With a catch in her voice, she loosely translated its inscription. "'And they who bettered life on earth by newfound mastery.'"

Alexander, who had been standing stoic and quiet at the foot of James' bed, openly sobbed. He'd always been a sensitive man, despite his lumbering height. And James had to wonder if, just like Josie, he recognized the pull from the other side that called to him so powerfully.

"Son, don't cry," he rasped. "Rejoice in the length of time we had together."

The air left his lips on a sigh. His energy dissipated. It mattered not. He'd lived a long and wonderful life, and now he was going to a higher place. He smiled and closed his eyes, hoping his family could hear what he did. "The angels, they sing."

"James!" His family chorused his name.

He sucked in a breath, but somehow it didn't collect in his lungs. "Believe," he whispered, his soul slipping away. "Believe . . ."

He stood barefooted in sun-warmed sand, watching Alexander and a chubby James Junior kick the soccer ball around. Their shrill laughter was snatched away in the crisp sea air, drowned out by the noise of the foaming swell. But their joy was palpable, and Robyn and Marina grinned beneath the shade of a striped umbrella as they unloaded the contents of a picnic basket onto a big blanket.

The temperature dropped. Antiseptic stung his nose. He looked down. The many-times scrubbed hospital floor glared with the reflection of overhead lights. Marina was asleep on the hospital bed, and just beside her, her newborn baby snuffled with dreams.

Then moonlight rippled over water—the lagoon, the falls a ceaseless background noise. He stepped forward, towards the couple wrapped in each other's arms and sound asleep. He frowned. Surely that wasn't Marina and . . . him? A stick broke underfoot. The couple stirred.

Suddenly he was standing in the open doorway of Robyn and the professor's patio, smoky cooking scents tantalizing in the air. The professor flipped a steak on his barbecue, his free arm tugging Robyn closer to his side. He smiled down at her, love and adoration so open his stare. "You have to be strong. You have to keep the faith."

James was running, so free and so young! African children were racing beside him, big white grins on their faces as they tried to keep up. Such a simple activity, but how these children lived!

Suddenly he was a young boy, frantic as he raced up to Josie who was crouched beside Maxwell.

"I'm bad. I'm bad," she sobbed.

The moment he wished he knew the whole story, the scene before him instantly rewound and then played forward in slow motion.

Josie walked through the shadowed white form of Molly, totally ignoring her outstretched hands to stop.

Josie threw the ball for Maxwell. It sailed high out of the yard, bouncing onto the street. Maxwell gave chase. A blue car screeched around the street corner and motored towards Maxwell.

The dog froze right in the middle of the road.

James closed his eyes at the impact, at the look of horror on his sister's face.

"Oh, Josie," he whispered. His heart sank for her. "You were trying not to believe in Molly, just like Mom and dad told you."

And you paid the price.

When he opened his eyes, he was in a big room—his parents' living room. He saw himself at the end of the big twelve-seat table, a triple-layered chocolate mud cake in front of him and eight candles burning bright.

Josie sat next to him, quiet and withdrawn in her frilly party frock and hair up in ribbons. His Mom sat at the other end of the table, severe in unrelenting black.

"Well, blow out the candles, James, what are you waiting for?" his Mom said harshly.

"Daddy—"

"Won't be here. Just . . . blow them out."

James stood back, feeling for the small boy he'd been. There were no friends, no happiness, and no fun. Just a duty-bound mother and a sister too intimidated to enjoy even the cake.

James wondered what went through his mother's head, as she watched her eight-year-old boy blow out the candles, a single tear sliding down his cheek that he couldn't quite hide.

His stomach lurched at a sudden shift in memory.

He was standing in a hospital. His dad, so young and vibrant was clutching Margaret's hand. Shock hit him in the solar plexus at the realization his Mom was giving birth. To him.

A hundred other emotions swirled freely in the room, and hit him one after the other. Excitement. Anticipation. Elation. Love! He felt them all as his dad took hold of the slippery baby and cut the cord.

Then James was suddenly floating, looking downward and watching a polished coffin winched slowly into its final resting place in the ground. His family stood solemn and teary eyed around the gravesite, their attention wholly on the coffin.

Josie stood back a little from the rest, her silver-grey hair now cut short. She held the aged poetry book in her hands as she looked up and smiled.

"James," she whispered. "I never got to read you a poem before you left us."

Marina looked up sharply, her attention now all on Josie. "He's here?" she asked, almost desperately.

Josie nodded, conceding gently, "I believe he is." Then she opened the pages of her poetry book, and read in a clear, beautiful voice.

It all comes down to this . . .
This time, this place, this now.
You . . . born from intimate love avowed
A creation beyond belief, nothing amiss.
God's greatest wonder, greatest gift.
Born into a world
Where life's path is long travelled
Destined friends, places, and events unraveled
A rocky trail or one straight; unfurled
It's your choice, which path to the new world.
Though each step in faith that's taken
Isn't always your fastest route ensured
There is an end to all sufferance, please be reassured
Understand you've not been forsaken
Just sleepwalking . . . till the moment you awaken
As dust is to dust

And the earthly curtain drawn
Love given and love received lives on
Beyond our reckoning, in a greater cause we trust
Promises fulfilled for the faithful and the just.
~Mel Teshco & Kylie Sheaffe

He saw a telltale flush of goose-bumps prickle Josie's skin, even as he absorbed her wonderment, one that matched his own.

It all made so much sense now.

His family, Marina, the professor, and Robyn—even Tom and Stevie, all had been an intricate weave, a coming together of his life's journey. Every step along the way, every new friend he'd made, all had been an inevitable, preordained rung in his learning, his life experiences.

Marina sobbed, her shoulders shaking with anguish. James was suddenly beside her. But as he tried to comfort her, to lay a hand on her tear-trekked cheek, his gossamer touch became a shadow passing through her solid form.

Of course she couldn't physically feel his touch. And yet, she seemed to sense his presence when she whispered, "James," and clasped her hands over her chest, her heart.

"Goodbye, my love," he said gently.

A beam of light radiated from his heart, dazzling through her hands and into her own heart, warming her, giving her strength. Though she couldn't see it, James knew she felt his presence, took comfort from the gift he'd bestowed.

She smiled then, a wobbly, loving smile. "Thank you," she whispered.

Everything abruptly swirled, and he was alone with the vibrant colors muting around him. Shadows danced in the mix, until darkness momentarily eclipsed all else. Complete, utter blackness. Complete silence.

What is happening to me?

Brilliant light abruptly filled his vision. There was no more darkness, just an endless blanket of white, where love, peace, and tranquility abounded all around.

This isn't death. I feel alive.

Like a fog swept aside by a breeze, a towering, craggy mountain emerged right before him. And in that moment he knew without any doubts, it was time to conquer it once and for all. He had to scale his Everest, to climb to its highest, rocky peak.

Not a chance. I'm just an old, frail man. I can't possibly make it.

Something bright snared his attention high above. He craned his neck. A dazzling rainbow arced over the tallest peak, beckoning. Then he heard the words, "No James Edward I know ever gives up."

His pulse jerked as he squinted, peering high above. "Professor?" But his voice echoed eerily into the emptiness.

In his peripheral, he could see a growing darkness beneath. An infinite void. He had the most overwhelming sensation he had to avoid heading down that way, at any cost.

Shivering, he looked downward, only then realizing he stood on a single step, seemingly in midair. He swallowed hard and squeezed his eyes shut, whispering, "I understand now. I have to have faith." He opened his eyes, his soul rejoicing at this complete and utter understanding. This . . . truth. "I Believe."

At that moment, a stream of molten silver surged down the mountainside towards him. He didn't flinch, didn't baulk. Where once fear had resided, purity of faith now reassured.

The stream stopped just above him, forming a perfect step alongside the mountain, becoming part of it. But pure and shining.

He stepped up onto it, his breath wheezing like an old, wounded warhorse, his muscles jamming tight. And yet, somehow he felt lighter, freer. "I believe!"

More molten silver rushed down the mountainside. Another perfect step formed, higher above him. A grin pulled at his lips as he heaved himself another step upward. Then another and another.

Closer to heaven.

His breath came easier, bone-deep weariness sliding off bit-by-bit as he ascended. And though the summit was still such a long way off, exhaustion was no longer a hairsbreadth away.

Pebbles clattered down from above, a shower of dust following in its wake—and yet he remained untouched. He looked up, scarcely believing his eyes.

A man toiled on the face of the mountain, seemingly hanging on by sheer force alone. He was using a pickaxe, painstakingly chipping away at the rock, cutting out a foothold so that he could climb all the way to the top.

Compassion cut James to the quick. He might be dead, but he wasn't unfeeling. "I can help you," he yelled.

Immediately, the loud strains of "Somewhere over the Rainbow" played, drowning out his offer.

James frowned. He reached up, stretching. "Here, take my hand!" The music volume blared. James pulled his arm back and covered his ears.

The man above continued on, deaf and blind to James' offer and ignoring the music as though immune to its significance, its sound.

He won't accept your help.

James looked around. The music was at ear-splitting volume, and yet those words had filled his mind with a clarity that had him acknowledge unconditionally, it had come from a higher order.

Only when James understood that and he continued up the stairs, did the music stop. It was then that he noticed a darkness surrounding the man, an evil shroud that attached itself to him like a foul smell.

And James knew this man had a long, arduous climb ahead.

It was only as he left the man far behind, the steps solidifying before him faster and faster, did he become aware of the spring in his step, his effortless stride.

He looked down at his sun-spotted and wrinkled hands. His skin was now smooth and unblemished, his hands those of a much younger man. "Thank you, God," he breathed, awed by this divine gift.

And as he climbed, he saw more souls, all at different levels along the mountainside, all with the same goal to reach the summit.

The rainbow visibly brightened, dazzling the eyes. Then it seemingly crystallized before exploding into a thousand droplets of brilliant colors, raining all around him.

He broke into a run, each step forming as fast as he could go as he bound up step after step. Laughter spilled free at the sight to behold so close.

He stilled at last, staring in wonderment at the bright, glorious figure taking form right before his eyes.

A verse from the Book of Matthew popped into his mind. And he was transfigured before them. And his face did shine as the sun, and his raiment was white as the light.

Like a child, James broke into a run, straight into Jesus' open arms, into his embrace of immeasurable love. Pure light radiated outward to encircle him. Minutes . . . Hours . . . Days . . . Infinity. James couldn't be sure of the distance of time, just that this unconditional love was as long as it needed to be.

He was whole now. Complete. Without worry, without pain.

"Thank you, Jesus," he whispered again, and stepped back to gaze upon his face, to absorb his presence.

But then he saw Molly, a much younger version of Josie, approach. He felt a tear of joy slide down one cheek when he realized his Mom and dad were either side of Molly, their arms around her as they walked towards him, each of them smiling.

Though his parents were as young as he was now, there was instant recognition. An ageless bond.

They silently embraced, no words necessary for this magical and special moment.

Only then did he see the much younger professor and his wife, Robyn. They emerged from nowhere, their hands clasped as they approached, smiles plastered on their faces, too.

Next came Leonard and his daughter. Leonard was slim, healthy, his daughter beautiful, radiant, and carefree.

His granddad walked towards him, and Kaye soon followed.

Everyone he'd known and lost began to gather around him, their spirits bound to his, each a special thread in the colorful tapestry of his life.

Then, in knowing silence, they all turned and stepped beyond the curtain of dazzling whiteness, each passing through a spectrum of color. Red, orange, yellow, green, blue, indigo, and violet. And out into the lush Garden of Eden that awaited.

Josie opened her eyes with a tender smile. She pushed her poetry book shut, the sun glinting on the embossed gold lettering on its cover, highlighting the title.

AWAKENING.

She bent, and with frail hands she placed the book beside her brother's fresh burial site.

As she walked away, a sudden breeze flicked open the book, riffling its pages. Her smile stretched into a grin. "I'll be seeing you soon, my dear James."

"James. Wake up, darling."

His eyelids jerked open. When his wife's still-youthful face looked down at him with nothing short of warmth and love, his heartbeat slowed its gallop and the dream faded.

No. Not a dream. He'd just seen his future. An epiphany.

He'd never been surer of anything in his life.

"Sorry to wake you after your all-nighter at the hospital, but you have a phone call." A wry smile curled his wife's lips before she sat on the mattress beside him. "And it sounds important."

He sat, gathering his thoughts even while fragments of the dream still lingered. Lifting a hand, he gently scraped a strand of her glorious hair from her face before leaning in, his lips brushing hers.

Nothing was more important than his wife. And he'd spend the rest of his life making sure he never took her for granted.

Ever.

Ten minutes later, the phone call disconnected, he turned slowly to face Marina.

He barely focused on the hand she put to her mouth and her eyes that had widened on seeing his expression. His focus centered on her other hand that was pressed to her belly, swollen with child.

Their child. The girl—daughter—he'd seen in his future.

"James, what is it?" she breathed, evidently reading his dazed incomprehension.

His stare lifted, taking in her anxiety. "It's nothing." He dragged a hand through his hair. "And it's everything."

She stepped forward. "Tell me."

He wondered abstractedly at the sense of loss coming over him when he said neutrally, "I received an offer from an old colleague."

"Offer?"

"Yes. Doctor David Lowe. He asked if I'd be interested in moving to Africa."

It'd mean helping change other people's lives. Making a difference. Doing what he loved, what he dreamed.

He blew out a breath and shook his head. He couldn't expect his family to uproot their whole lives to satisfy his own wants. "But it's mostly voluntary work deep in tribal country. Of course we can't go—"

"Why not?"

He paused, taken aback. "Our baby."

"Oh, James. You see and yet you don't you see. What matters is that our baby grows up in a society where nurturing and love are considered normal; where money is barely relevant and what's real is real. We couldn't ask for a more worthy gift for our child."

James looked at Marina with a love and respect he could barely contain. "And Alexander?"

"Will love it, too."

James closed his eyes for a moment, taking it all in. He'd seen his future, knew he and his wife would live to a ripe old age, surrounded by their loved ones.

So why the reservations?

Marina's touch on his forearms was soft and persuasive. "Everything you told me about your last trip to Africa sounded amazing. It seems as if we're meant to go there. Besides, as long as we're a family, everything will work out. You know it will."

He nodded and she continued gently, "It's past time you overthrew all those doubts in your head and went with your heart."

You have to decide whether to follow your head or your heart. The professor's wise and all-too-similar words echoed in his head as though in approval.

His hands found their way to her shoulders when he asked, "Do you remember what you said to me all those years ago at the falls?"

She nodded, her smile warm. "How could I forget?"

"You trusted that I'd take care of you. And I took that seriously."

"And you've proven your trust." Her smile was full of wonder. "And when we move to Africa, I know you will keep our family safe."

He pulled her close, the love he felt for her more than he could put into words. He could only try. "There's nothing that love cannot face. I will take care of you and our children, now and until my last dying breath." He kissed her then, long and slow, his stare shining with adoration. "Sweetheart, that's one promise I know I'll keep."

Sometimes I wish I had great big wings

To rise above my troubles;
To clearly see soaring through the heavens,
One of God's angels, who joyfully sings.
Sometimes I wish I could just let go
Of the cares and worries I cannot solve
I could give and live as God had planned
And then the good times would surely flow
Sometimes I wish I could simply forget
All the things that caused me pain
The stuff that cut deep in my heart; my soul.
Once and for all, letting go of my regrets.
Sometimes I wish I could make a difference
World hunger, poverty, and war.
Children would smile; a tear would be wiped,
Life lived, empowered by benevolence.
Sometimes I wish I had eternal youth
In a haven where death itself ceased to exist.
Waterfalls of colored love and endless light
Wash away all darkness, for an eternity of truth
I can . . . for God gave me love"
~ Kylie Sheaffe & Mel Teshco

Want more? How about a romantic suspense novel from Mel Teshco?

Dimensional

What would you do, if you had the chance to revisit all your decisions, to fix all your mistakes?

Celebrity chef, Jessie McCormick is incredibly late. Driving his Hummer to the opening of his latest restaurant seemed like a much better idea than flying, but incomprehensible directions and a dodgy shortcut throws him instead into the driveway of a rickety old house. Hopeful of finding the house occupied – and its inhabitants capable of directing him to Brisbane – he heads inside.

What he finds inside that house will turn his perspective inside out and upside down and change his life forever. Voices lead him to an attic, and there he finds no direction and every direction. The attic is an endless line of doors and ladders, each taking Jessie down a different path of his life.

His dimension is just one of many, with each one uncovering alternate realities. In one a beautiful country cook becomes his lover and the one woman he can't stop thinking about. In another his sister is in danger and his long-dead mother is alive. As Jessie races to find his way back to his own dimension, he must make the biggest decision of his life: rescue his sister or take his chance at true love.

Dimensional available HERE[1]

---

1. https://www.amazon.com/dp/B09NJXJZYQ

Chapter One of Dimensional

Jessie McCormick peered through the dust-caked windshield of his Hummer, negotiating the rutted and narrow track that followed the perimeter of an old barbed wire fence.

According to an aged mechanic who'd fueled his car at the one-horse town of Mirraway, this unsigned, unsealed road would cut over an hour off his journey to Brisbane.

A pity the track ended just ahead. He slowed the SUV and blew out a harsh breath, the knots between his shoulder blades not loosening even a little as he caught sight of a shabby old house between weedy looking shrubs and towering gum trees.

He rolled down the automated window and decelerated as he scanned the landscape with a frown. No birdsong filled the air and no breeze stirred the leaves, which drooped from yet another dry and relentless Australian summer. His frown deepened. There was something unsettling by the stillness outside, a quiet that was almost unnatural.

A flicker of unease hovered in his gut. He'd been so caught up in navigating the track and worrying if he'd make it to the opening of his twenty-third restaurant that he couldn't pinpoint exactly when the world outside had begun to feel different. It was as if he was an insect in a bottle, disconnected somehow from humanity.

He shook his head and ignored a sudden compulsion to spin his vehicle around and make a quick getaway. For god's sake, he was a thirty-five-year-old man, a chef at the pinnacle of his career; he would not let his imagination go off the rails now!

He cut the Hummer's engine, closed his scratchy eyes for a couple of blissful seconds, then opened the door and climbed out. All he wanted was help to get out of this cursed countryside and back to civilization. Somewhere he could use a landline phone, or better yet, somewhere he could get mobile coverage and perhaps even make it yet to his latest restaurant acquisition.

He peeled off his too-hot jacket when flailing wings abruptly broke the thick silence that was as palpable and suffocating as the midday heat. He dragged in a steadying breath, his pulse resuming normal rhythm on seeing the big crow that had settled on the rusted tin roof of the house.

At least he wasn't alone.

"Great consolation," he muttered, before tossing his jacket onto the back seat. There was no air conditioning out here and no one to appreciate his tailored suit. He could have worn a pair of old shorts and thongs and been a hell of a lot more comfortable for it.

The door clunking shut behind him, he cut through the stringy, long grass littered with the concrete shards of a broken path. He glanced up at the crow, the bird staring down at him with a glittering eye.

"What are you looking at?"

The crow's one eye blinked and Jessie snorted at his own idiocy before he continued to the front door, stooping for a moment to swipe off the sticky grass seeds clinging to his pants.

"Hello!" His voice echoed emptily in the still air.

The sun beat down on his bare head, uncomfortably hot. He loosened his tie as sweat dribbled between his shoulder blades, his shirt sticking to his back. All that heat yet his insides steadily grew chilled, as though he was intruding on hallowed ground.

He dragged a hand over his face. The rising temperature was making him lose the bloody plot. He rapped on the wooden door with its peeling green paint. "Is anyone home?"

Of course there was no answer; he hadn't really expected one. The only thing to greet him was the sudden hot breath of wind that rustled the dry gum leaves like rusty castanets and clapped a loose piece of old tin somewhere on the roof overhead.

He glared up at the cloudless azure sky. If it wasn't for his unhealthy fear of flying, he wouldn't be in this position. He'd probably even now be celebrating his good fortune with his colleagues.

He turned away and took a step toward his SUV.

"Hello."

He froze, his heart jumping out of his chest. He must be going stark raving mad. Because whoever had called out from inside the house had a voice that was unmistakably his own.

Not. Possible.

With a disbelieving, impatient hiss of breath he spun back to the house. He didn't bother knocking this time and the doorknob turned easily under his hand, before he pushed open the door with just a moment's hesitation.

A musty dankness hit him first, followed by mousy-smelling urine and feces. It was dark inside, the lone cracked window beside the door filthy and half covered by a latticework of spider webs. But even with the gloomy interior it was obvious this was the only room in the tiny house.

Whatever innards had been inside the house—cupboards, sink, pantry—were there no longer. It was just a shell. Whoever lived here had probably used an outhouse for a toilet and an outdoor shower from the sketchy water supply of a corrugated iron tank.

Whoever *had* lived here had probably died half a century or more before.

He was most definitely alone.

He shook his head. "I really am an idiot!"

The soughing wind had been all he'd heard, surely? It was the only logical explanation he could come up with. He'd always been the rational one out of all his peers, not to mention his family.

An old mustard-colored chair, half its stuffing spewing free from the back of the seat, lay awkwardly on its side. Jessie's scornful laugh echoed in the room, disconcerting and a little unnerving.

Get a grip, man. It's just an old house.

He jigged the chair back onto its legs before sitting and dragging a hand through the prickles of his close-cropped hair. "A fine mess I've got myself into," he mused aloud, watching as a large, seedy-looking cockroach ambled across the torn linoleum floor that was faded to a mottled puke green.

He leaned back in the chair, ignoring its creak of protest and the headache creeping upon him as he closed his eyes, his head lolling backwards.

His eyelids snapped apart a nanosecond later at the indistinct muttering of somebody's voice—just as another blast of hot air had the loose piece of tin flap again overhead. Only then did he notice the large square hole in the ceiling.

An air vent? No, a manhole.

He froze. A chill trickled up and down his spine, his gut clenching. Had the voice come from the ceiling? Because it hadn't been his imagination this time, he'd definitely heard someone.

A shiny aluminum ladder—Jesus, had it been there earlier?—was perched against the edge of the hole, looking totally out of place with its shabby surrounds.

He jerked to his feet, the chair clattering back onto its side like marbles hitting iron as he edged his way toward the ladder. He trusted his senses, they'd gotten him out of a whole shitload of sticky situations and right then they prickled with foreboding.

It hadn't been the fault of an overactive imagination. Nothing in this place could be taken for granted. Nothing could be fully believed.

He'd take a quick look to satisfy the questions rattling around in his head and churning in his gut, then he'd hightail it out of there and return the way he'd come. No harm done...aside from his credibility and a small fortune.

Taking a deep breath he began climbing, half afraid the ceiling would crumble from his extra weight. It stayed intact, and his relief was twofold when he looked up to discover the darkness in the ceiling was broken by a shaft of sunlight pulsing through the loose piece of roof iron.

His head breached the ceiling. The hairs on the back of his neck rose. *"Holy shit."* He swallowed past a suddenly parched throat as a soundless rush of denial tore through his brain.

The roof stretched endlessly either way, lit every few yards by an identical shaft of sunlight streaming through what appeared to be the very same loosened piece of tin, like an infinite line of mirrors. And in the ceiling below, a row of square holes, each one revealing the top of an aluminum ladder.

"I don't believe it," he said hoarsely.

He glanced into the room below. The cockroach was still ambling across the floor, near the chair that lay keeled on its side, the seat innards beside it. Everything seemed so normal down there. Up here, he questioned whether he just might be losing his sanity.

But the seemingly immeasurable roof cavity couldn't be real. It had to be a trick of the light, or his imagination. His heart thumped as though a drum in his chest and he closed his eyes for a couple of seconds, willing composure. He had to take a better look, or forever doubt his own eyes...his own logic.

Gritting his teeth, he clambered onto the ceiling and crouched low on its rotting rafters. The tin above his head flapped again, echoing loudly either way in a further chorus of bangs.

Senses jangling and skin crawling, he carefully balanced his way across a beam, peering down into each room he passed with stunned incomprehension. *Impossible!* The rooms below were identical.

He looked behind at the infinite roof and ceiling, and the endless row of manholes. Dread suffused him from the inside out. Fuck. Which hole had he climbed through?

He thrust an unsteady hand over his face, striving to make sense of the unexplainable. And failing.

His breath hissed. It didn't matter anymore. All that mattered was that he returned to the room he'd entered and get the hell away. He shivered, his breath bursting in and out as unholy terror crept into the base of his skull. No longer was he the hard-assed man whose tough ethics preceded him.

Not since his mother's death had he been more frightened.

Swiping his sweaty palms on the seat of his trousers, he inched back the way he'd come, wishing now he'd thought to count the manholes that he'd passed. But one room would connect to another, right?

He couldn't be sure of that, he couldn't be sure of anything. Not in this place.

Gripping hold of what he guessed was the ladder he'd climbed, he carefully descended and dropped onto the floor. He released a taut breath and looked around. He was definitely alone here, he didn't doubt that now. And he'd swear this was the same room he'd been in earlier.

"Only one way to find out." His voice echoed eerily, emphasizing his aloneness.

Striding toward the grimy window, he swiped a hand over the pane and looked through the smudged mark that was now marginally cleaner. He took a step back, his shoulders loosening with relief. His bright yellow Hummer was just where he'd left it, yards from the front door.

Thank you, god.

Something moved in his periphery. He turned, watching as a sickly looking cockroach started a familiar, slow trek across the room.

It's a different roach...a totally different fucking roach. But the unsettled feeling within shot into a whole new stratosphere of hysteria as he all but sprinted for the front door and jerked it open.

If you would like to know when Mel Teshco's next book is available, news, cover reveals and more, you can sign up for my newsletter: madmimi.com/signups/121695/join

Check out my website – http://www.melteshco.com/

You can also friend me on Facebook at https://www.facebook.com/mel.teshco

Or on my author Facebook page at https://www.facebook.com/MelTeshcoAuthor

And occasionally on Twitter at https://twitter.com/melteshco

Contact me: melteshco@yahoo.com.au

If you enjoyed our story we'd be delighted if you would consider leaving a review. This will help other readers find our books.

About the Authors

Mel Teshco loves to write scorching sci-fi and contemporary stories with an occasional paranormal thrown into the mix. Not easy with seven cats, two dogs and a fat black thoroughbred vying for attention, especially when Mel's also busily stuffing around on Facebook. With only one daughter now living at home to feed two minute noodles, she still shakes her head at how she managed to write with three daughters and three stepchildren living under the same roof. Not to mention Mr. Semi-Patient (the one and same husband hoping for early retirement...he's been waiting a few years now.) Clearly anything is possible, even in the real world.

Kylie Sheaffe once a burdened spiritual intuitive, Kylie has learned to embrace her inherited gifts, unleashing their healing capacity, extraordinary insights, and unconditional love. Being real and approachable with her quiet wisdom, she offers a world of unexplored potential.

Books by Kylie Sheaffe and Mel Teshco

Awakenings: series order

No Ordinary Gift

Believe

Homecoming

Books by Mel Teshco

Contemporary:

Desert Kings Alliance: series order

The Sheikh's Runaway Bride (book 1)

The Sheikh's Captive Lover (book 2)

Coming soon

The Sheikh's Forbidden Wife (book 3)

The Sheikh's Secret Mistress (book 4)

The Sheikh's Defiant Princess (book 5)

The VIP Desire Agency: series order

Lady in Red (book 1)

High Class (book 2)

Exclusive (book 3)

Liberated (book 4)

Uninhibited (book 5)

The VIP Desire Agency Boxed Set (all 5 books in the series)

Box sets with authors Christina Phillips & Cathleen Ross

Sheikhs & Billionaires

Taken by the Sheikh

Taken by the Billionaire

Taken by the Desert Sheikh

Resisting the Firefighter

Standalone longer length titles: (50k-100k)

Highest Bid

As I Am

Standalone novellas and short stories: (15k-40K)

Stripped

Clarissa

Camilla

Selena's Bodyguard (also part of the Christmas Assortment Box)\

Anthologies:

Down and Dusty: The Complete Collection

The Christmas Assortment Box
Secret Confessions: Sydney Housewives
Science Fiction:
The Virgin Hunt Games volume 1
The Virgin Hunt Games volume 2
The Virgin Hunt Games volume 3
Coming soon
The Virgin Hunt Games volumes 4-6
Dragons of Riddich: series order:
Kadin (free prequel - book 1)
Asher (book 2)
Baron (book 3)
Dahlia (book 4)
Wyatt (book 5)
Valor (book 6)
The Queen (book 7)
Alien Hunger: series order
Galactic Burn (book 1)
Galactic Inferno (book 2)
Galactic Flame (book 3)
Coming soon
Galactic Blaze (book 4)
Nightmix: series order:
Lusting the Enemy (book 1)
Abducting the Princess (book 2)
Seducing the Huntress (book 3)
Winged & Dangerous: series order
Stone Cold Lover (book 1)
Ice Cold Lover (book 2)
Red Hot Lover (book 3)
Winged & Dangerous Box Set (all 3 books in the series)

Dirty Sexy Space continuity with authors Shona Husk and Denise Rossetti:

Yours to Uncover (book 1)
Mine to Serve (book 6)
Ours to Share (book 8)
Standalone longer length titles: (50k-100k)
Dimensional
Mutant Unveiled
Shadow Hunter
Existence
Standalone novellas and short stories: (15k-40K)
Identity Shift
Moon Thrall
Blood Chance
Carnal Moon